Fire & Brimstone

Stella Williams

Book Cover by Luna Noire

Developmental Edit by Erica Gentner

CopyEdit and Proofreading by Raw Book Editing www.rawbookediting.com

First Edition 2023

Content Warnings

This book contains content related to manipulation, stalking, and violence.

Contents

1. Once Upon a Time...   1

2. Tale as Old as Time   13

3. Off the Market   21

4. Twist of Fate   32

5. Tempted to Touch   42

6. A Low Blow   56

7. A Real Piece of Work   64

8. Only Time Will Tell   71

9. Dark Night of the Soul   81

10. Once Upon a Dream   94

11. Gather the Troops   104

12. Sundown Showdown   110

13. Happily Ever...   118

Also By Stella Williams   123

Once Upon a Time...

The bartender set three shots in front of Cerrita and DJ. One for Cerrita and two for DJ. Cerrita wasn't much of a drinker. She couldn't be, not with Desmon obsessively stalking her. As it stood, one drink was getting a little too comfortable than Cerrita should allow. Yet, almost six months in Mulberry and he hadn't tracked her down yet.

She'd been a little scared when a couple of small fires popped up in the last few weeks, but none of them had fit Desmon's usual MO. He set fires to get her attention, fires that were out of the way and wouldn't do any real damage to people and buildings. Still, she couldn't shake the feeling that he was close, so there she was out on the town with her friend DJ.

She'd spent too many years letting Desmon and her family control and manipulate her. She was beyond over it. She smirked thinking about how they would react to seeing her now, her once flowing locs now a short pixie cut. No ornate make up to sculpt her soft rounded face into sharp angles and edges, just thick sticky lip gloss and mascara.

Hell, even the little black dress she wore would send them into a fit as they preferred her to be wrapped in the finest silk and softest cotton. Okay so that part she did miss but not the rest. Shaking her head to chase away thoughts of the past, Cerrita grabbed the neon pink shot and tossed it back. The cherry flavored vodka burned her throat and nose. Her face must have shown her discomfort because DJ shook her head and patted Cerrita's back.

"Really, Rita? We need to work on your tolerance if you want to cross drinking buddy off your list," she said, swinging all 30-inches of her rainbow-colored wig over her shoulder.

When preparing for the evening DJ had offered to let Cerrita borrow one of her many colorful going out wigs but Cerrita had declined. Not only was she done with long hair but she couldn't afford to replace even the cheapest of DJs collection if something were to happen. Not to mention standing out wasn't something Cerrita wanted to do, despite being friends with one of the flashiest people on earth.

"It's fine. I think that one is officially off the list."

"Noted. Let's move on to the next item on the docket for tonight." DJ scanned the crowd, a much easier feat for someone of more average height. They both wore 4 inch stilettos but that still meant Cerrita barely reached her friends shoulder in height.

"Dancing?" Cerrita asked hopefully.

"Of course," DJ said with a wink.

Cerrita groaned before allowing DJ to drag her out onto the dance floor. Not for the first time, Cerrita questioned herself for opening up to DJ about her bucket list. She'd made it after her two month mark in Mulberry. Staying in a larger city was much easier to keep hidden than in the smaller towns she'd attempted to stay in. For one the humans weren't nearly as nosy and the supernatural community was much more diverse. Your specific type of Supernatural wasn't as important or as defining. The relative anonymity she enjoyed in Mulberry allowed her to hope again. Being on the run was getting old, and if Desmon was going to catch her, she wanted to live first. She wanted to experience life to its fullest, not the carefully constructed cage her family and Pack had put her in.

Making a friend had been top of her list, and DJ had excitedly filled that role for her. Cerrita wasn't so easily trusting, but DJ had proven herself trustworthy in multiple ways since they first met. Starting with helping Rita with a custom pheromone blocker to hide the fact she was a Phoenix. Most people would have used that knowledge against Cerrita. They would have demanded payment in feathers of Phoenix fire, but DJ never asked her for any of those things.

Now months later, DJ had helped Cerrita fulfill almost everything on her list. A night out drinking and dancing with friends was one, but the other reason DJ dragged her to the dance floor was to help Cerrita attract a potential mate. She didn't need a true mating, but it would at least be nice to have a connection with someone who wasn't after her for power or money.

DJ grabbed Cerrita's hips and moved them with the beat. "Loosen up, girlie! Just have fun."

"Right, fun," Cerrita reminded herself, releasing the tension in her muscles and letting the hypnotizing beat guide her movements.

"Whoo! Look at you!" DJ said, fanning herself.

Cerrita laughed and let herself get lost in the music. Drinking may not have been her thing, but dancing seemed to be just the right kind of fun for her.

The Afrobeats floating through the club should have put Terrence Shaw and his brothers in a better mood. It was a rare night off, and they'd chosen to enjoy a night out at one of the popular human clubs. A couple drinks and a night in a willing female's bed were just the thing to distract them from the growing pile of open case files on their desks.

Yet here they sat, killing the vibe in VIP. The bottle of CasaMigos at the center of their table was empty, another already on its way. Their fun night out was quickly turning into a tense drowning of their worries in booze, not broads. Not that there weren't options. Six women had approached them so far, offering to satisfy their physical needs, but none garnered more than a half-smile from the three men.

"I'm going to take a leak," Terrence muttered to his brothers before forcing his body from the leather couch.

His brothers grunted as a response. He made his way to the public toilet, made quick work of his business, washed his hands, and headed back to the bar. He'd settle the tab and drag his brothers back to the office. That's where their minds were, anyway. Only as he was waiting for the bartender to bring back his card, he noticed the other setting a row of shots in front of the most radiant woman he'd ever seen.

The cautious smile she gave the bartender wiped Terrence's brain of anything but the thought to find out more about her. She toasted with the woman next to her before tossing back the shot. Then her face scrunched up and her tiny hand raised to her elegant throat. He was about to come to her rescue when the bartender came back with his card.

"Just need you to sign this and then you're good to go," the bartender said.

It was only a few seconds for Terrence to sign his name and shove his card into his wallet, but that seemed to be enough time that his firefly had disappeared into the crowded club. It was probably for the best. She had an innocence about her, something he'd clocked even at a distance. Even if he had approached her, she would have probably run screaming in the other direction.

Yet, he couldn't help searching for her in the crowd as he made his way back to VIP. Her petite stature and demure style made it nearly impossible to spot her amongst the undulating mass of bodies. He'd just reached the roped off area when he spotted her. She was in the middle of the dance floor, moving her lithe little body to the beat. Her eyes were closed, her face relaxed and thick shiny lips curled into a blissful grin. If he thought she was radiant before, now she was glowing. He wasn't the only one who noticed. He watched through narrowed eyes as three other men made a beeline toward her.

Before he could blink, he was pushing through the crowd toward her, too. Only one man had beaten him to her. He paused, watching the interaction, watching how she flinched when the man touched her before spinning around, her small hand curled into a fist.

The man put his hands up in mock surrender with a smarmy smile on his face as he bent to talk to her. Terrence found his own fists balling up as she tilted her head back to giggle at whatever the man had said. He wanted to be on the receiving end of that smile. He wanted to be the one causing the delightfully airy bubbles of laughter. He was so caught up with his own uncharacteristic thoughts that he didn't see the man's smile falter as the woman turned away from him and started to dance again. Only this time, she didn't close her eyes. They were glued directly on Terrence.

Cerrita had felt the heat of his stare on her before the sleaze boy had touched her. She'd reveled in it, let it wrap its way around her body and settle nicely in her core. She didn't need to look to know he was there. She'd been aware of him since before her failed drinking attempt. Call it paranoia, but Cerrita always made note of her surroundings before allowing herself to relax even a tiny bit in public.

She'd clocked him sitting with two other men in VIP. Their presence was dark and malevolent, but she'd sensed they weren't out to cause trouble. Then she'd seen him settling his tab at the bar. She'd thought he would leave, but here he was, watching her. It should have been unnerving, but it wasn't. It was empowering to know that without even trying, without him knowing her secret, he was drawn to her.

The heat he shot her way was enough to garner her Phoenix's attention, and that was why she made no move to approach him. Her Phoenix's interest complicated things. Even in a human club, Cerrita couldn't risk taxing the limits of DJ's genius pheromone blocker recipe. Cerrita could keep herself in check but she'd never had to deal with her Phoenix being aroused as well, the risk of her scent being released and revealing her true nature to any nearby Supernatural was too much.

So no, she wouldn't approach him. And would walk away if he approached her because as much as she wanted to feel a genuine attraction to someone, she was scared. Scared she would enjoy it a little too much, reveal a little too much, and put her life and his at risk because he could make her hot, even from a distance. With barely a glance.

"Rita, if you don't go over there," DJ hissed in her ear.

Cerrita opened her eyes and shook her head.

"It's too dangerous," she replied.

"He's dangerous all right, but that type makes for the best nights," she encouraged.

Cerrita bit the inside of her cheek before hazarding a glance in the man's direction. Long thick locs draped over his broad shoulders and framed a face chiseled from the gods. As soon as their eyes met, she knew the decision had already been made. Cerrita Powell was about to have her very first one night stand.

"Fuck, okay. I'll drop a pin on my location."

"Don't forget to use protection," DJ said with a wink.

DJ didn't just mean condoms. Black market pheromone blockers that masked or hid the mating scent of a shifter were now part and parcel of the casual dating scene. Safe sex for most shifters in the city meant also protecting oneself from unwanted claims. Something Rita was overly aware of. Which was another reason she was grateful her friend was such a skilled alchemist. She may play the role of flighty party witch, but DJ had her secrets too, one of which was the recipe for her super potent pheromone blocker.

Cerrita patted her purse. "I brought two just in case."

Shaking her head, DJ pushed Rita forward. "One should be enough, but for your sake, I hope you get a two bottle experience."

Rita resisted the urge to roll her eyes at her friend. Making eye contact with the man again, she made her way through the crowd.

The club seemed to move in slow motion as she walked toward him. He found himself moving to meet her half way. Like a moth drawn to a flame, he reached for her. She took his hand and allowed him to pull her flush against his body.

"Care to dance," he breathed.

His little firefly shook her head. "Take me someplace private."

His cock jumped in his pants, almost as high as his eyebrows, at such a forward request.

"Are you sure? You don't even know my name yet." He couldn't help but question.

"Names are overrated," she said, and he laughed.

Any other woman and he would have already declined, but something about her screwed with his usual voice of reason.

"Can I call you firefly?" he said instead.

"Only if I can call you beast," she replied.

He made a face. "Do I look like a beast to you?"

The woman appeared to truly think about it for a second before smiling and nodding. "Like a fairy tale. I want you to whisk me away and make me forget I have a real name."

That settled it. He was in way over his head already, but if he were drowning, he'd gladly do it while giving her exactly what she asked for.

"Fuck, firefly. Follow me."

The one shot of vodka had gone straight to her head. That was the only explanation for the things that had just come out of her mouth. Honestly, in what fairy tale did the male lead make the heroine forget her name? None she had ever read. Still, her words had done the trick.

She was on her way out of the club with a sexy as fuck behemoth that made her fire dance like a hurricane lantern.

She'd never felt this uninhibited before. Never felt the tingling excitement that coursed through her like electricity through copper wiring, fast and full of energy. If she wasn't careful, the electric feeling could put her in a terrible spot, but she didn't quite care at that moment. She was living, finally living, and she had a feeling a night with this man could be the thing that finally sets her free.

Beast held her flush against his front as he guided her out of the club. The chill of the night air hitting her body did nothing to quell the heat inside her. It only added a layer of sensation, a contrast to the gentle warmth of him at her back and the burning desire at her core. His large palm rested on her hip, and she purposely exaggerated the swing of her hips so his thumb drifted under her blouse to skim across her bare skin with each movement. A small innocent touch, but it acted as further kindling for the arousal building within her.

By the time they reached what she assumed to be his blacked-out SUV, Cerrita wasn't sure she would make it to a second location. Before he could open the door for her, she spun around, wrapping her arms around his neck, and she dragged him down so her mouth could reach his.

She'd only meant to get a small taste of him, but as soon as her lips were against his, he slid his tongue past them and delved into her mouth. She sucked at his tongue while he stroked her mouth. She hadn't realized how sensual a kiss could be, her only experience with it having been a sloppy wet disaster of a kiss with her current stalker. This kiss, however, there were no words, only feelings. Soft feelings, rough feelings, pleasurable feelings that made her forget they were in a public parking lot while she climbed him like her favorite tree back home.

Just like her favorite tree, she could barely wrap her legs around him. His grip shifted from her hips to her ass, kneading her cheeks and pressing her hard against his thick erection. He moaned as she rocked her hips against him. His grip tightened, keeping her flush against him as she rode him faster and faster until the electricity zipping through her concentrated at her core and exploded into a million fireworks.

"Beast!" she cried out against his lips.

"That was just the beginning, firefly. I'm going to have so much fun with you tonight," her beast said, slowly lowering her jellied legs to the ground.

"There's more?" she gasped, looking up into his eyes.

He bit his lip and pressed a gentle kiss to her forehead. "Fairy tales have multiple chapters, firefly. They have twists and turns, high and lows, but most importantly, they have a climax. This one will have multiple if you're up for it."

Cerrita's eyes widened at his implication, but her heart only raced faster. Without a second thought, she dug out a bottle of her pheromone blocker and sprayed herself down with it. Her beast waited for her to finish before leaning in close and taking a deep sniff at the crux of her neck and her shoulder.

"I understand the precaution, but you've rid me of my prize."

"Your prize?" she squeaked. Her old fears cut through her arousal. Had he been able to catch her scent through the blocker? Was her secret exposed? Would he try to force a mating claim? The panic must have shown on her face because he took a step back, his arms falling to his sides.

"Is something wrong?" he asked with concern clear on his face.

Something told her lying to this man wasn't a good idea, but she also couldn't exactly tell him the truth.

"Thanks for the ride, beast, but I think I'll have to pass on the rest of the fairy tale." She rushed away before hightailing it back to the club.

Didn't anyone ever warn her not to run from a predator? The hunter instinct in him wanted to give chase, but he held back. Something he'd done had spooked her, but he was, in fact, more of a gentleman than a beast. Still, the loss of opportunity grated on him just as much as his curiosity was piqued by his mysterious firefly.

Maybe she really was a firefly. Dawn was approaching and her light had dimmed as night came to a close. Shaking his head, Terrence pulled out his phone and texted his brothers that he was outside waiting. He would have loved to text them that they needed to find their own ride, but that ship had sailed. It was time to put his enforcer hat back on.

As he tucked his phone away, he noticed something on the ground wedged almost out of sight by the front wheel, the slim metal atomizer his firefly had used to dispense her pheromone blocker. It was nondescript, for the most part, with a matte black finish, but on the bottom was a symbol he couldn't quite place. He knew he'd seen it before, just not where. All he knew was it was unlike any blocker he had ever come across before. Could this be the same one hindering him and his brothers from solving many of their recent cases?

The vial felt light in his hands, and he couldn't feel anything sloshing inside. It was probably empty, especially the way she'd showered them both with it. Either way, he'd hand it to Harvey later. Maybe he could salvage a few drops to see if this was the blocker getting in their way.

The worst part was because of this blocker, he'd been unable to catch his firefly's scent. He could probably still find her inside, but after the way she had fled from him, there was little chance she would be forthcoming about her supplier. His best bet would be to track down the symbol, and maybe if the fates were gracious enough, they would give him a chance to capture his firefly and give her the fairy tale fuck she deserved before he let her back out in the wild.

Tale as Old as Time

One Month Later

Desmon Burrage glared down at the city from above, the cool glass of scotch in his hand quickly heating to a boil as he searched the streets below. His anger built as he sensed his woman somewhere just beyond his reach. The only thing keeping him from actively searching for her was business he had to handle. The city's lights were too bright, but Desmon could still smell the tang of smoke in the air. Smoke from the fire he'd set on the property of his business partner's rival.

"Do I need to remind you where you are?" a dark whisper said from his left.

Desmon looked up and glared at Kevin Kerrigan. The hotel's owner and his gracious host during his stay in Mulberry. Desmon would be gladly received by the area's shifters, but didn't want to expose his hand to those greedy bastards. It was better to deal with the devil than risk losing track of his Phoenix now that he'd finally gotten her in his sights again. It was too late to seek help from the shifters now that he'd set fire to the Pack leader's estate. A warning from Kevin and a calling card for his flighty Phoenix mate.

"Your physical possessions are safe as long as you make good on your part of the deal," Desmon muttered, taking a sip of his now lukewarm scotch.

Kevin chuckled and pulled an envelope out of his suit jacket. Desmon reached for it, only for Kevin to snatch it back .

"Don't forget the second part on your end."

Desmon grit his teeth as he pulled the silk handkerchief holding three of his plumage feathers from his pocket and handed them over to Kevin. His grip tightened on his drink at the man's self-satisfied smirk, fingering the red and black feathers Desmon had plucked from his own plumage just a few hours earlier. One feather was more than enough for any ritual purpose. Three was excessive, too much power for any man, but Desmon had learned Kevin was much more than a power-drunk human. He was touched by a daemon. The darkness was deep in his bones, and Desmon had seen firsthand just what the dark serpent could do when unleashed.

Kevin tucked the feathers away before handing Desmon the information packet. "Your mate is gorgeous. I should have charged you more for this information."

Desmon snatched the packet from Kevin and tore into the tan envelope. Ready to confirm the information presented to him. Inside was all the information he needed to lure Cerrita into a trap she couldn't escape. The anger inside him dissipated and his Phoenix pressed against his skin, ready to be set free.

"Once I have my mate, I hope to never need your services again." He didn't give Kevin a chance to reply before allowing the shift to overcome him. He circled once around Kevin's head before disappearing into the night sky.

Dodging high rises, the Phoenix soared through the city. The flames dancing along the red and black feathers on his back casting ominous shadows around him as he scanned the streets below. She was here in Mulberry. Kevin had confirmed it, but she continued to evade him. Five years of this cat-and-mouse game. She belonged to him. His right was to claim the golden Phoenix and bring her to heel before him. She would mate with him and produce his legacy. He would be all-powerful with his golden Phoenix by his side. Whether or not she comes willing, Cerrita would be his.

Om.

Cerrita released her breath before breathing in through her nose and repeating the calming chant. The smell of smoke tickled her nose, and not from the fragrant patchouli burning beside her, but the acrid tang of a structural fire. The stench broke through her calm, scrunching her nose. Cerrita fought the urge to sneeze. She slowly blinked her eyes open to look out the picture glass window of her living room. Outside, a thick brown haze obscured her view of the city lights.

The fires were getting closer, and she could feel the call of the dancing flames urging her forward. Urging her off her mat and away from her morning meditation. She slipped on her sandals and headed out the door without a second thought. Acting on instinct, she slipped into the alleyway between her home and her neighbors', using the shadows to disguise her shift as best she could. Then she was airborne, her golden yellow and orange feathers spreading wide and taking flight. She circled as close to the flames as she dared. Too close and she wouldn't be able to control her own flames. If she danced with the flames, it could possibly spread the inferno raging into the field beyond the flaming garage of the massive estate on the outskirts of the city.

On top of the heat of the flames, her skin was abuzz with energy, letting her know shifters inhabited this property. Shifters who employed magic wards to keep out unwanted visitors like herself. Although the local shifters knew she had moved to town, Cerrita had purposely avoided all invitations to join the Mulberry Pack structure. Being a rogue shifter wasn't ideal, but Cerrita craved her freedom. Freedom from the spectacle her life had been when under Pack rule.

Her gift was also a curse. A Phoenix born to a family of falcon shifters, a rare mystical form only gifted once every couple decades to one male and one female. The male Phoenix cannot create another Phoenix without mating another Phoenix, but the gene is still passed with hopes of another Phoenix in the future. Another reason she was content with being rogue and hiding out in Mulberry, far away from the only living male Phoenix.

Every Pack wanted her as a shiny trophy to hold up as a sign of their good fortune. A fortune that would be made off her back, quite literally. The sale of her feathers, the ritual use of her flame. Let alone if she were to mate another Phoenix. The thought made her shiver despite the warmth of the flames below. Any thought of Desmon Burrage was enough to send her running in the other direction. Hell, she'd been running for the last five years. Away from the familial pressure, the pressure from her Pack, and from Desmon himself.

They'd been friends once. As kids, they'd played side by side, flitting through the clouds, setting small fires here and there before dousing them with gusts of wind kicked up from their beating wings. A friendship she'd remembered fondly until she'd overheard him and her own father discussing her like a piece of meat. Like she already belonged to Desmon. His property.

What she had seen as mere play had all been a sick plan to make her more at ease with their eventual mating. A test of her abilities and how easily she would heed his direction. When the Pack Alpha had congratulated Desmon for his cunning instead of upholding the Pack laws about forced or manipulated courtship, Cerrita had had enough. She packed a bag and took off.

First, to a neighboring Pack to seek shelter, but they'd only coveted her feathers and flame. They locked her away under the guise of protecting her until they could reach an agreement with her Pack. Two years under lock and key until she'd freed herself. Then she'd begun wandering as a rogue, never staying in one place long enough because Desmon always found her.

It wasn't until she'd stumbled into Mulberry that she'd finally found a place he couldn't track her. The city had too many different Supernaturals, too many places with heavily layered wards that, even if he caught up with her here, she had plenty of avenues to evade him. So, even if this fire gave her the heebie-jeebies, if it reminded her too much of Desmon's flame pattern, if he'd somehow managed to find her this time, she wouldn't run.

There was no place else to run, and that meant she was going to do what myth said could not be done. She was going to have to kill a Phoenix.

Terrence Shaw scowled at the charred remains in front of him, shaking his head. The flames from last night's fire had finally been doused with a combination of spelled firefighting gear and enchanted water.

"Phoenix fire," Harvey grumbled, wiping soot from his face. Still decked out in his firefighter gear, he shouldered two rolled up hoses.

Terrence let out a shaky breath. As a Hellhound, fire wasn't usually a concern for him and his brothers but Harvey looked like he'd just been put through the ringer. Phoenix fire would explain that rare occurrence. It would also explain why the regular fire protections in place hadn't put a dent in the inferno before Supernatural help arrived. Terrence glanced over to where his other brother, Sampson, was gathering statements from the staff. From the scowl on Sampson's face, he wasn't getting any clearer of a picture on how this happened than Terrence was.

They were on the property of the Pack Alpha. His prized vintage car collection was nothing more than a pile of ash. Nothing had survived, not a frame, not a brick. Literal millions of dollars, now dust and ash at his feet while the pristine lawn just inches away showed not even a bit of char on the tips. That would have stumped any human investigator, but despite Phoenixes being few and far between, with enough money and connections on the black market, you could get your hands on a little Phoenix fire.

Not enough to do this much damage, though, and usually one would want to recover their fire before it was extinguished. That meant they were usually nearby and easily apprehended. The person who'd done this not only had massive quantities of Phoenix fire but an unheard of overstock that was impossible to fathom. That could only mean one thing. They were dealing with a real live Phoenix, and as far as he was aware, the only two currently alive were happily sequestered in one of the southern Packs.

Terrence stood and walked over to Sampson. He tapped him on the shoulder. "Have any Phoenixes registered in the area recently?"

Sampson scowled at Terrence like he'd just spit on him. "If there was, do you think I'd be down here taking statements instead of hemming them the fuck up?"

Terrence shook his head. "Well then, it looks like we have a freak rogue Phoenix hunt."

The backlog of cases currently on their desks had all of them in a bad mood. To add a rogue Phoenix to the equation was literally throwing kindling on a fire already dangerously close to being out of control.

"Not without the boss man's say so," Sampson grumbled, lifting his chin toward the main house. Sure enough, as if summoned by the mere mention of himself, Gregorio Linux slunk toward them in a monogrammed silk pajama set and matching leather slippers. His thin face pinched into a scowl that looked more like a petulant pout. Behind him strode one of his pets, a human lawyer named Elias Westmoore. To be fair, Elias was more than a pet, he actually served a purpose. He managed the Pack's legal affairs and helped keep Supernatural crimes out of public knowledge.

"Who would dare do this?" Gregorio ground out. The 'to me' didn't have to be added.

Gregorio might look like a pampered dandy, but the man wouldn't be in his position if he weren't just as lethal.

"The evidence points to a Phoenix."

Gregorio scowled, "Impossible."

"Probable," Terrence countered.

"There is only one Phoenix in the area that I am aware of, and they wouldn't dare do something like this," he sniffed.

Terrence raised an eyebrow at the Alpha. It didn't surprise him that Gregorio would know about a Phoenix in the area who wasn't registered with the Pack.

"You have a name for this Phoenix? It's best we check all leads," Terrence said.

Gregorio bent down and conferred with Elias in whispers. Terrence could have listened in, but his caution outweighed his curiosity. Sometimes ignorance really was bliss, even in a high-profile arson case.

When Gregorio finished whispering with his lackey, he straightened and turned back to Terrence. "Do your job and bring me the culprit directly." With that, he turned on his heel and marched away. Elias Westmoore, however, lingered behind.

"I'll make sure the local news reports this as an accidental chemical spill or something. Give you a little more time to get ahead of this arsonist. In the meantime, perhaps you should take a night off. Visit Club Hellfire, ogle the servers. Who knows when you will get the chance once this investigation is in full swing."

Terrence shook his head. "You really suggesting that I take a night off just when this mess is tossed in our laps?"

Elias sighed heavily. "Go, you never know what wonders a little break can do when handling a case such as this."

It dawned on him then. Elias wasn't telling him to slack off, the man was trying to give him a lead on this Phoenix the Alpha obviously didn't want them to track down. Once again, Elias proved he was more than just Gregorio's pet.

"Thank you. I'll consider your advice."

"Good," the man said before turning and following the Alpha.

Off the Market

Cerrita sniffed at herself and scowled. No matter how long she showered, the smell of ash clung to her skin. A frustrating reminder that all her running had done nothing but delay the inevitable.

She would have to face her tormentor sooner rather than later. He was getting more aggressive in his pursuit, dangerously so, and Cerrita knew she could never allow him what he wanted. She could never allow him her body or her power.

In order to do that, though, she needed a concrete plan. She needed insight on how exactly to get rid of a Phoenix for good, and for that, she would need help. Being on the run didn't exactly lend to making friends, but Cerrita had let her guard down a little here in Mulberry. Now, instead of being a total loner, Cerrita had DJ.

DJ was all magic and light. She could turn almost anything into a party. It was her love of life that had drawn Cerrita to her and, as Cerrita had learned, DJ had never met a person she couldn't call friend. It was one of the ways Cerrita hoped DJ could help. She knew a lot of people from all walks of life. Surely, she would know someone who might be able to put Cerrita on the right track to find a way to get rid of Desmon. Cerrita pulled out her phone and opened their running text thread.

C: You busy?

DJ: Just about to open the shop.

C: Good. I need a refill on my pheromone blocker.

DJ: A refill already?

C: Yeah, I picked up a night shift.

Cerrita hoped DJ wouldn't press for more of an explanation than that. Technically, Cerrita had enough to cover her general needs for the next week, but if Desmon was close, she would need to double up her stash. Not just to keep him from tracking her, but to have on hand in case her plan failed and she was forced to leave the first place that had felt comfortable after her world came crashing down around her.

DJ: I can have it ready in about 30.

C: Great! See you soon.

Cerrita tucked her phone away and went over to her closet where she kept her go bag. Unzipping the black canvas duffle, she rummaged around inside until her fingers made contact with the soft leather binding of the book she'd stolen when she'd left home. The leather warmed in her hands, the thin detailing channeling her Phoenix energy into the magical lock coded only for a Phoenix to open.

"Show me how to defeat Desmon," she whispered, and the book flipped open several pages to the section about mating.

Cerrita sighed. She'd read through this section a million times, hoping to find some hint at a loophole in the language. At this point, she knew it by heart. Female Phoenix were powerful creatures, but their purpose was solely to mate one of their own and to help their male counterpart unlock their full power. Basically, sacrificing themselves and their power to their mate. It made Cerrita's skin crawl just thinking about submitting to Desmon. Of giving Desmon any more power to justify his overinflated ego. She ran a finger over the embossed painting that accompanied the damning message from the only guidebook she had. Two figures locked in what was depicted as a loving embrace, surrounded by a whirling mass of Phoenix fire. Instead of appearing romantic, it reminded Cerrita of a depiction of Hell on earth.

"I know about mating, but that isn't going to save me. I want to be rid of Desmon," she implored the book again.

The book lay unmoved in her lap. With a curse, she shoved the book away from her. She shouldn't have expected anything different. This wasn't the first time she'd asked the book for help, but now she was certain that whoever had charmed the book had a very clear motive for what was included.

At least, it wasn't her only option. Someone, somewhere, had to know something more about Phoenixes and how to get rid of one. To find that person, however, Cerrita needed the help of her friend.

The Saturday morning market crowd would provide a cacophony of different smells, wards, and unsettling magic to mask her presence if Desmon was searching for her. She took a deep breath and steeled herself to the onslaught before stepping forward and into the fray. The market itself wasn't all that extraordinary. At least, on the surface.

It was, in fact, a human farmer's market, where farmers and crafts persons hocked their wares. Three rows of tiny carts, ten-foot canopies, and trunks filled with fresh fruits, vegetables, and home-made concoctions made up the bulk of the market, but that wasn't what Cerrita was there for.

She headed past the tempting edibles to the last row that backed up to a row of small storefronts. The original part of the market. The old strip mall had been bought out by Supernaturals over the years. Many of the businesses remained the same—a barbershop, a laundromat, a dry cleaner, a meat market. There were a few at the end of the row designated as metaphysical supplies. It was there Cerrita was headed. Not to the larger store with the line coming out of its two front doors, but the one right next door. A small sign on the glass door read Jourdain Alchemy 2nd floor.

Cerrita pulled the door open and took the three flights of stairs two at a time until they opened to a small space crammed full of shelves and cases that held all manner of oddities and potions.

"Be with you in a minute," DJ called from somewhere toward the back.

"It's me, DJ," Cerrita called back.

"Well, in that case," DJ appeared from behind a tall curio cabinet. Cerrita shook her head as she saw her friend tuck a peacock feather into the fold of her emerald green turban, right next to the dazzling peacock pin that held the fabric together.

"You didn't have to get all fancy for little old me," Cerrita teased.

"Oh please, you know I only dress like this for the tourists," DJ replied before coming over and giving Cerrita a hug.

Disa "DJ" Jourdain was Cerrita's first and only true friend. When Cerrita had first arrived at Mulberry, DJ had saved her from a scammer selling a fake pheromone blocker. Cerrita had almost been conned out of her last fifty bucks, but thanks to DJ, not only did she get what she needed but DJ also got Cerrita a job waitressing at one of the clubs she occasionally deejayed for. That's right, DJ was an alchemist by day and DJ Alchemy by night.

"You got the good stuff?" Cerrita said after returning the hug.

"Girl, you know I do, but why the urgency? You just bought a bottle last week and should have more than enough to get you through another week, at least, even with picking up extra shifts. Unless you're finally taking my advice about getting you some."

Cerrita wanted to roll her eyes but refrained.

"I thought I saw my ex the other day."

DJ's eyes narrowed. "Thought you saw or saw saw?"

"Think. It was like an out of the corner of my eye thing. Anyway, I just want to be on the safe side."

"You know, if you would just tell me his name, I could have some people keep an eye out."

An almost smile crept onto Cerrita's face. Another thing she loved about DJ was she didn't pry. She could have easily figured out that Cerrita was running from another Phoenix, and a simple search of the shifter index would bring not only her name, but Desmon's as well.

"No, this is my problem, but I could use your help with something else."

"Like what? Hooking you up with a sexy badass who will keep you in orgasms and your ex at arm's length?"

"That would be nice, but no. I need to get my ex off my back both figuratively and literally."

"And I keep telling you that maybe getting under someone else is the cure you need, but you know I'm just a silly little party witch," DJ laughed.

"When I'm ready, it will happen, but for now, I just need some information on Phoenixes."

DJ snorted. "Really? What about your little manual?"

"If there was anything in there that could help me, you know I'd have done it by now."

"Honey, if this man is really that dangerous, I think you need to take this to the authorities." DJ's demeanor shifted from playful to concerned.

"My ex doesn't want to kill me; he wants to possess me, and he's used Phoenix fire to get his hands on me before. I just want to be prepared if I have to fight fire with fire, you know?" Cerrita explained.

DJ eyed Cerrita for a bit before sighing heavily.

"I still think you should seek the protection of the Pack if you are really that scared."

"So, you aren't going to help me?"

"I'll do my best, but please say you will think about going to the Pack about this." DJ stood back to her full height and waved her hand toward the various wares around the small shop. "I think my dad might have a book somewhere that has a few Phoenix potion recipes, but as far as an expert, you'd have to travel to one of the Phoenix-marked Packs."

Cerrita scowled. She couldn't do that because that would mean going home. Her Pack was the only Phoenix-marked Pack left.

"Thank you for your help. If I thought the Pack would do anything but make this whole thing worse, I would go to them. I can't trust that they won't accept his false claim on me, since he has my family and old Pack backing him."

DJ snorted. "You shifters get on my nerves with your repressive rules about mating. They've done one good thing by enforcing the law against forced physical markings, but that has only made scent marking more of an issue. Either way, your no should be enough. Another reason I feel you should reconsider this whole celibate act you've got going. He can't force a mating on you if you are already linked with someone else."

"I have considered it, but why take a chance on causing a repeat situation when battery powered buddies will get me there without all the fuss?" Cerrita said.

It had been a while since she was intimate with another person. Her first and only encounter was with the guy she'd met at a human club last month, and could she even really count that? She hadn't even shared with DJ what really happened that night. When she'd run back into the club, she'd told DJ she chickened out. It hadn't been a lie, but she'd been too embarrassed to admit she literally rode the man fully clothed in the parking lot before getting triggered and bolting. That experience, while great, had shown Cerrita just how unready she was for mating in general. She'd been sheltered by her family under the guise they were looking out for her. When in reality, they had been preserving her for him, for Desmon. It was bad enough she had allowed him to be her first kiss, but was eternally grateful she hadn't succumbed to his pressure for more. Especially now that she knew the truth about him.

"Do more than consider it. You've surely got enough blocker to make sure nothing sticks, not to mention this extra you requested," DJ said, pulling the slim silver atomizer from her skirt pocket.

Cerrita reached for it, but DJ held it back. "There anyone you have in mind? Someone who has piqued your interest? Let me know when you find someone you find interesting. This city can be smaller than people think, especially in the Supernatural community. I can tell you if he'll be worth it."

Cerrita did roll her eyes this time. "No one in mind. I may as well have blinders on."

"Take them off, honey. Slip on a pair of rosy shades and get you some joy. I've known you for almost a year now, and the only time I've seen you relaxed is after your meditation sessions," DJ said.

"It's hard to relax when you have a literal target on your back," Cerrita muttered.

"What you need is someone to put you on your back. How long has it been since you got your back blown out? Do you even know how to properly use the pheromone blocker for such an occasion?"

Cerrita ignored the first question, and while she knew that back breaking sex was supposed to be good, she couldn't fathom how. If your back was broken, wouldn't that be painful and possibly life threatening? If that was the goal of sex, then Cerrita would take a hard pass. If she wanted to be broken, she would have stayed and mated Desmon.

"I know how to use it. I've heard from the other girls at Club Hellfire how to keep a claim from sticking."

"That's not what I asked, sweetheart."

"Spray myself down before and after, and if the male consents, spray him too."

"Girl, if he consents? Spray that sucker as soon as he walks through the door. Don't let caution get you caught up," DJ snorted.

"That is not okay. Consent goes both ways, DJ. He doesn't know what this is. He could have a bad reaction or something."

"And now you are questioning the quality of my product? I should kick you out right now."

Cerrita placed her hands on her hips. "It's not an issue of the quality. I'm just saying you decided to start adding fragrances last month. What if someone is allergic to those?"

DJ scowled. "I only use quality hypoallergenic ingredients."

Growing up in the south, Cerrita had seen quite a few reactions to citrus and had heard of cases of people being allergic to cinnamon as well. That really wasn't an issue for her. She had no plans to use it for anything but masking her trail from Desmon, even if she was going to let DJ assume otherwise.

"Are you going to give me the potion I ordered or should I go downstairs and get whatever will make do?"

"Now I know you're on some bullshit. No need to go after some inferior product, especially when I just upgraded my formula to have a light perfume to it. Just don't say I didn't warn you. Besides, if you find the right one, he'll have his own pheromone blocker handy right alongside any other contraceptive y'all use. Unless he's human; I don't recommend them, but they can get the job done if you're desperate," DJ advised.

"Definitely not desperate, but a fling with a human could be interesting," Cerrita said, playing along with her friend's assumption.

"Do what you're gonna do, but don't say I didn't warn you. Just don't forget that you need to apply a few pumps more than your average daily use to mask your activity."

"I won't. Anyway, where are you working tonight?"

DJ scowled. "K Lounge."

Cerrita made a face, too. She wasn't one to judge, especially since Club Hellfire wasn't exactly the safest place to work. But one thing Cerrita learned quickly upon arriving in Mulberry was any involvement with Kevin Kerrigan was a deal with the Devil. Nothing good could come from being under his employ.

"Is there something I'm missing here? I thought you would never get caught up with that..." Cerrita didn't know what to classify Kevin Kerrigan as.

On the surface, he seemed like any other spoiled entitled rich human, but there was an extra layer to him. A thick, oily layer so slick and sticky that even a moment in his presence left you marked with its oppressive darkness.

"Let's just say it was an offer I couldn't refuse and leave it at that. Besides, it's just one event."

"Mmhm, just let me know if you need help getting out of this obvious trap. I haven't used my one favor with Koda, and we both know if there is anyone who could possibly sway Kevin Kerrigan, it's him."

DJ shook her head. "Aww, you would use your one get out of Hell free card for me? I'm touched, but there is no need. I promise this isn't what you think. It's a private event, not related to that person at all except for the venue."

"Okay, but the offer still stands."

"Thank you. Now, back to the issue at hand. When was the last time you went lingerie shopping? I mean, aside from your work uniform, the sexiest thing in your closet is that gorgeous feather and lace gown you randomly own."

Cerrita shook her head. "Stay out of my closet. Thank you for the blocker, and I'll see you tomorrow for brunch?"

"Of course! You be careful out there, Rita."

Cerrita nodded and left her friend's shop. The market was even more crowded than when she first arrived. Even with the added crush of bodies, Cerrita still felt like she was being watched. She did her best to surreptitiously check over her shoulder every once in a while but no one really stood out to her. Still, she mingled amongst the crowd longer than she needed to and even doubled back to browse a few displays of rainbow-colored fruits and vegetables.

Eventually, she chalked her paranoia up to the recent fire. Desmon was close, but that didn't mean he had found her yet. She didn't need to alter her schedule because of it, either. She was tired of running, and the first step in her plan to end this once and for all was to get over this flight response to any hint he might be near.

Straightening her shoulders, Cerrita marched purposefully through the crowd. Refusing to shrink herself and scurry away. No, if he was the one watching her, Desmon needed to see she wasn't afraid of him. Not anymore.

Twist of Fate

Terrence tracked the movements of the young lady he'd seen slipping out of the smaller apothecary above the one he was staking out. It would only make sense that whoever was setting these fires would use a pheromone blocker to mask who they were. That had become basic criminal acumen in recent days. Phoenixes were rare and coveted for the power of their fire and feathers. There was no way one could walk around freely and without the protection of the Pack.

The crowded market made it harder to sniff out the Supernatural from the human, but this shop was the most popular because of the under the table sales of a generic blocker. It was a diluted formula, however, and required daily application, if not more. A small bottle would last a few days, a larger one for a few weeks. To mask one's presence while wielding Phoenix fire would require at least ten entire bottles of the stuff, meaning the Phoenix or the person in control of the Phoenix fire would be in need of a refill, if not now, then very soon.

Not for the first time, Terrence wished they would make the stuff legal so it could be regulated. It was one thing to mask who you were for safety reasons. It was another with the growing trend of masking agents to get away with crimes. This wasn't the first case low on leads thanks to the pheromone blockers sold by this location and possibly others.

Professionally, Terrence hated pheromone blockers since they made his job harder. Personally, Terrence didn't mind the idea of using the stuff to block unwanted claims. It certainly made casual dating that much easier. Not like he'd had time to indulge in any casual encounters, let alone date recently. His preoccupation with the brown-skinned beauty was testament to that.

Even with her suspicious activity, Terrence would have to be blind not to see her beauty. Her hair was cut short, leaving nothing to obscure the elegant length of her neck or her high cheekbones that tapered into the delicate roundness of her jawline. Wide brown eyes scanned the crowd as she walked. A slight pinch between her eyebrows and the tightness at the corners of her mouth were the only indication something was amiss.

Was she looking for someone? Had she been stood up by friends or a date? His eyes trailed her through the crowd. A petite figure with just enough curve to avoid being labeled boyish allowed her to weave through the tiniest of openings in the crowd. Her quick, decisive movements made a zigzag pattern that would make it almost impossible to keep eyes on her for someone not as trained as Terrence.

What are you running from, gorgeous?

He took a step in her direction, emerging from the shadowed corner he'd found to lurk in, and startled a young couple walking past. He nodded and smiled at the surprised pair before pushing forward and into the crowd. The woman had paused at one of the human merchants' stalls, admiring the rainbow of food on display. She was so close, but the growing crowd made it harder for Terrence's larger frame to maneuver.

Usually, his dark presence was enough to part any crowd, but today it seemed his inherent menace was no match for the enticing offerings at market. The crowd closed in for a second. He lost sight of her, and when it parted again, she was gone from the stall. With a curse, Terrence pushed further into the crowd, scanning the small openings ahead in the hopes of catching just one more glimpse.

Oomph!

Something solid smacked right into his chest. Terrence bit the inside of his cheek in frustration. He needed to find his little distraction before she was too far for him to catch her scent. Whoever just ran into him had cost him his chance. A big, black man bulldozing through a crowd was not the kind of attention he needed. So, he stopped and took a second to reign in his disappointment.

It was probably for the best that he'd lost her. For a minute, he'd forgotten why he was at the market. He didn't have time to think with his dick. He looked down, ready to apologize, but his words got stuck in his throat as his gaze collided with familiar brown eyes.

Quickly, he reached down to help her off the ground. "Sorry. Wasn't looking."

He studied her more, trying to figure out why she seemed so familiar now that they were up close. The woman's eyes narrowed as she studied him and then rolled her eyes. "No worries, it's crowded. I'm short."

Terrence frowned at her obvious instinct to shrink and submit and then frowned again because it shouldn't matter to him. He was here to try to find a lead. Yet, so far, this woman was the most interesting thing in the entire market. Even his inner beast had perked up at the sight of her. A rare occurrence for his Hellhound to be interested in anything other than doing its job of hunting down evil.

"That has nothing to do with it. Here, let me help you up," Terrence replied, but she ignored his offered hand and stood, shaking her head.

"I'm good. Thank you." She turned and darted off, disappearing into the crowd.

Terrence's gut reaction was to follow her, but duty came before all else. Before he went back to work, he bent to pick up the small metal tube the woman had dropped. That's when it all clicked. The fates had brought him his firefly. He smiled. With something personal of hers, he should be able to track her anywhere in the city. Not that he was going to. No, he would just find her to return her... Terrence studied the cool metal tube in his hand.

It was about the same shape and size of the packaging for pheromone blockers sold by the store he was watching, only this was obviously higher end. A custom blocker maybe. A quick glance at the bottom yielded no results, even being sold and traded under the table most establishments still labeled their wares. He opened the cap and took a sniff, expecting to find the same astringent smell as all the other blockers, only to be left with nothing but the faint essence of cinnamon and sweet citrus. Maybe not a pheromone blocker, but an actual vial of perfume. Even more reason to return it to her. Terrence pushed through the crowd, now able to pick out her scent trail thanks to her perfume.

Cerrita's heart raced in her chest, even after she escaped the congestion of the farmer's market. For a second there, she'd almost forgotten she was supposed to be lying low. That she wasn't in a position to be noticed by anyone. The way the stranger had sucked her in with the endless depths of his eyes and a smile that had nearly melted her panties off. The man had "look but don't touch" written all over him, and yet, she had been so incredibly tempted to do just that and more. Cerrita may have been a virgin, but she knew how to please herself, and this man was built straight out of her naughty little fantasies. Fantasies that should have been the furthest thing from her mind.

Damn DJ and her assumptions about Cerrita's sex life. Their chat earlier was the only reason Cerrita was reacting so out of sorts. Sure, the guy she'd run into was hot as fuck and seemed genuinely kind, but the paranoid feeling of being watched had increased twenty-fold as soon as their eyes connected.

It was like whatever danger meters she'd cultivated over the years had short circuited and instead of immediately triggering her flight response, had flooded her with something else entirely. Not just arousal, but an aching awareness that made her gut all fluttery. She had, however, been able to make her escape before making any more of a spectacle of herself. The stress of it all made her sweat, and the familiar scent of mahogany and spiced molasses with the undertones of a campfire tickled her nose.

"Shit!" she muttered, digging into her bag for her pheromone blocker.

She dug around until she felt the slim metal casing and pulled it out, ready to spritz away the scent unique to her, only for it to spray one pathetic puff of mostly cinnamon and citrus scented air. She must have used more than she thought last night after flying over that fire.

She reached into her purse again, thankful to have just stocked up and cursed herself for not getting two bottles instead of just the one.

Except, the brand new bottle she had just snagged from DJ was nowhere to be found. Cursing, Cerrita headed back toward the crowded market. It was the safest option to get back to DJ and spritz on one of her samples until she could get home where the rest of her stash was.

Terrence couldn't help the grin that spread across his face when he spotted his little firefly pushing back through the crowd in his direction. Apparently, she'd already noticed her perfume was gone, and he was more than happy to return it to her. Only, as he got closer, his Hellhound went on red alert. He wasn't the only one trying to reach her.

Through the crowd, Terrence saw three men in dark clothing closing in on her. The masses parted for them; their ill intent clear enough to even the most distracted human. Terrence had no idea why these men were after her, but he intended to find out, after he got to her first.

His own menace must have been showing as the crowd split for him too, and he had an almost unencumbered path straight to his destination, straight to her. Unlike before, his firefly wasn't paying attention to her surroundings and seemed completely oblivious to the trio of men approaching her. She kept her eyes on the ground, no doubt trying to retrace her path and find the vial he held clutched in his hand. His heart raced and a slight sheen of sweat broke out all over his body as he did his best to reach her before her other pursuers.

Terrence didn't have time to be bothered by this uncharacteristic panic. Panic that he couldn't reach her in time and those men would snatch her up and away before he could get to her. Before he could claim her because she was his.

That thought did give him pause, but it was too late. He'd barreled through the crowd and snatched her into his arms, holding her tight against his chest as he glared down at the three men at her back.

They all stopped and glared back, but not a single one made a move to get closer. The woman, however, squirmed against his hold and tried to say something that came out muffled against his chest. Belatedly, he realized he was probably crushing her with his strong grip, but the realization was only half of Terrence's problems. Her squirming had activated another part of his anatomy that quickly grew against her soft, warm belly.

Still, he held her there until he was sure the other men were gone. They faded into the crowd, and Terrence gave it another moment or two before he slowly loosened his hold on her. He didn't let her go, though, not yet, but he allowed enough space for her to look up at him with literal fire dancing in her eyes. Her hot, little body turned up the heat in a way Terrence had only ever felt when dragging an evildoer to hell. It was a good thing he was a Hellhound, otherwise, she could have actually hurt him with her heat. His clothes, on the other hand, wouldn't hold up much longer and the change in temperature around them wasn't going unnoticed.

"Mind turning the heat down a bit, firefly? Wouldn't want anyone to see just how hot we are for each other," he teased.

The fire in her eyes blazed brighter before being doused completely. Her wide expressive eyes fluttered closed and the surrounding temperature dropped back to the meteorologist confirmed temperature of before, only instead of nice, it felt like he'd been plunged into the arctic. He missed her heat, but the chill did wonders for rectifying his inappropriate hardness.

Cerrita took another deep, calming breath. She may have been able to reel in her fire, but her heart still threatened to jump out of her chest. The beast. He'd found her. The weight of his arm resting just above her ass wasn't helping,. How could she not have recognized him sooner? She needed to get out of his arms, away from his maddening touch before... Cerrita didn't want to think about her reaction to him.

It was so much worse now than the first time that she'd felt his skin against hers. Her body and her Phoenix were painfully aware he was thick and hard in more ways than the obvious and hadn't flinched at her heat. She didn't want to think about why she hadn't used her self-defense skills to disable him and make her escape, or why she hadn't screamed or thrown a fit to get help in front of the humans in the crowd. Most of all, she didn't want to think about how safe and secure she felt in his grasp, her Phoenix completely at ease.

Fuck, if she were a cat shifter she'd be purring and rubbing herself all over the man. This stranger. Her stranger. Her beast.

She took another deep breath, slowly releasing it to the count of ten, and then she opened her eyes. The world moved around them as if they were merely a tree or another trash can to avoid while perusing the goods. At least, she didn't have to worry too much about being seen. It appeared they were invisible to everyone around them despite being smack in the middle of a busy walkway, which was perfect except now the hint of mahogany and spice was more like someone had burnt Christmas cookies in their general vicinity.

Shit. Shit. And triple shit!

She needed to get to DJ's to rectify this fast. She forced herself from the beast's grasp. "I need to go. I…"

He smirked down at her and held up the metal canister she'd been looking for. "I was planning to return this," he said and held it out to her.

She snatched it from his grasp and quickly doused herself with more than enough to cover her scent and anyone else who happened to be within ten feet of her. The bottle was half empty by the time she felt neutralized enough.

The man watched on with an amused smirk. "So, it is a blocker? I'm not familiar with this formula. Is it custom?"

Cerrita eyed him warily. On one hand, she'd love to give her friend some new business, but on the other, she didn't know this man from Adam. Not only that, but he had to know what she was after that scent bomb she'd just dropped and the slight loss of control she'd had with her Phoenix fire. Maybe she should offer to take him to DJ's and see if she had a memory wiping potion Cerrita could slip into his atomizer instead.

Yes, that was what needed to happen. Maybe she could take some of the memory potion too and forget she ever ran into the literal man of her dreams while on the run from the man of her recurring nightmares. Cerrita pocketed her half empty atomizer and cocked her head toward DJ's shop.

"I'm going to need another refill. Why don't you follow me to the shop?"

"Sure. I'm Terrence, by the way. Terrence Shaw." The man nodded and extended his hand to gesture her forward, even as he kept the other firmly on the small of her back.

"Ugh, don't tell me your name! We agreed to no names," she breathed and moved towards her friend's shop. She may have been able to put distance between their bodies, but he seemed insistent on keeping some form of hold on her. It was beyond her to protest it, even as he tucked her possessively against his side.

Tempted to Touch

F irefly made her way quickly through the crowd as if she were trying to run away from him, or at least put space between their bodies, but Terrence wasn't having it. He'd come here in the hopes of getting a lead on his arson case, and Firefly had been a pleasant if confusing surprise. A Phoenix who was successfully navigating the world as a rogue. One who still refused to tell him his name. She probably had a million secrets he'd have the pleasure of uncovering. At least, as long as he could keep her by his side.

She moved quickly through the crowd like a bird slipping between air streams. Of course, keeping up with Firefly didn't mean he had to touch her, but he justified it because of the crowd they waded through.

"So, what do you do?" he asked, trying to break the silence.

Firefly kept moving forward and ignored his question. She obviously didn't plan on sharing anything more with him. Annoying but smart. He should have expected her to be fairly tight-lipped. She wouldn't have survived a day as a rogue without keeping personal details private.

"We're almost there," she finally said.

Terrence nodded, even though she couldn't see it as he was positioned at her back at the door to the stairs leading to the apothecary, where she sourced her pheromone blocker from.

Going up the stairs was going to be torture. He'd have no reason to hold on to her in the narrow stairway, but if he were too far behind, he'd have a glorious view of her swaying ass at just about eye and mouth level. That would be too much of a temptation, even for Terrence. He never thought of himself as inherently creepy until the opportunity was right there in his face.

Especially as she took the first two steps up. That was when his phone started to buzz in his back pocket. He ignored it the first time, and the second, as he followed her up the stairs. The swaying of her hips slipped him into a horny trance that made him want to grab her by the waist and bury his face there until she was riding his face and screaming his name. His real name, now that she knew what it was.

Thankfully, his phone buzzed a third time, saving him from embarrassing himself. He knew it was too important to keep ignoring. Even if he was following a lead. His little firefly was a Phoenix, and she was about to introduce him to the person who could either make or break his case.

He didn't want to believe the first woman to grab his attention so thoroughly was the one who set the fire last night, but he could not shake the feeling she was involved somehow.

Not just because she was a rogue Phoenix, had a custom and highly effective blend of pheromone blocker, and was being followed by three men who were obviously hired guns. Which now he wasn't so sure they were after her, or rather just doing their jobs. It was possible she hired them for protection. Being a rogue Phoenix couldn't be easy, but then, they had backed away without checking with her. Maybe she just thought she was rogue and her Pack or a loved one had hired them? There were too many variables, and it all was a distraction— his attraction to her, the men following her, this new apothecary selling a blocker so powerful one spritz had been enough to kill any trace of her scent mark after she'd doused him with it.

Fuck, what he'd give to be covered in her scent, to roll around in it, to savor the taste of it on her skin. His phone interrupted his train of thought once again. He blinked twice, realizing they had arrived at the front door. He was so close, and yet again, duty called. He pulled out his phone and cleared his throat.

"Sorry, I have to take this," he muttered and took a step back from Firefly and the door.

"Oh, that's fine. I'll just be inside." Firefly looked up at him, and the relief in her face was almost enough to douse the inappropriate thoughts running through his head. Almost, because while the human part of him knew thinking and doing were two different things, his beast, his hound, howled and clawed at him from the inside, angry they were no longer touching her. That Terrence was putting distance between their two bodies.

Claim her!

Own her!

Make her ours!

Its very bold and inappropriate statements repeated in his head. His beast was a literal hound, give it a scent, drop it a bone, possessive and obsessive were in its nature. Yet, it had never uttered a peep about Terrence's human proclivities until Firefly. He couldn't be sure if his hound was suddenly so obsessed because Firefly was fine as fuck and could stand the inherent heat of Hell and possibly more, or was it because her Phoenix would make a good snack?

It's just for a minute while I answer the phone.

Terrence pasted on a smile and watched as Firefly went inside before he answered his phone with a rough growl, "What is it, Harvey?"

"Whoa, did I catch you at a bad time? You need a little more sleep before doing actual work?" Harvey said flippantly.

"I'm following a lead. What do you need?"

"There's another fire. Me and Sampson are on our way to the scene now. What's this lead you're following?"

"I found a Phoenix."

"A Phoenix? Not *the* Phoenix?"

"You said you are on the way to a fire. I've been with this Phoenix for at least a half hour, so she can't be our arsonist, but I have this gut feeling she is connected to all of this somehow."

There was some rustling on the other line before Sampson's deep baritone came through the speaker on his phone. "Stick with your lead. We've got this scene handled."

The call disconnected before Terrence could say anything more. On one hand, he was grateful he didn't have to leave Firefly's side just yet and she clearly wasn't responsible for the fires, or at least, not this one. Maybe one of those goons he'd seen following her had set the fire to throw off the investigation? Either way, he had plenty of cause to keep tailing her until he figured out just how much she was involved with all of this.

Desmon circled the market where Cerrita had last been spotted. The team he'd sent to bring her to him had failed at their jobs. Incompetent fools! Not worth a single one of his feathers, let alone the three he had forked over to Kerrigan to secure their use. They claimed that with the enforcer involved, they were out. Snatching an innocent girl was one thing. Going up against a Hellhound was another. Desmon scoffed at their cowardice.

A Hellhound would be the least of their worries once he had Cerrita back.

Even now, being this close, he could feel the surge in his power, the pull of her fire beckoning him. It was exhilarating, intoxicating. He wanted more. No, needed. He needed more of the glorious power their union would give him. Just this little taste of what the future could hold was like a pure shot of adrenaline to his system. Even now, he had to restrain himself from barging right into that building and dragging her out in the street to claim her and his power in a way that could not be contested.

All of this was an unnecessary inconvenience. He'd given Cerrita enough time to herself. He'd waited patiently for her to come of mating age, courting her the proper way. Now here he was, exposing himself, chasing her around the country and using up valuable favors. Enforcer presence or not, Desmon was far too invested now to back down. The enforcer they spotted her with should be long gone chasing the fire he'd left as a distraction. But neither had left the building they'd dodged into after the men he sent had been seen.

The rational part of him knew he should just leave. There would be more opportunities to grab Cerrita now that he had found her. The enforcer was a complication he had not counted on. Kerrigan's intel had mentioned nothing about her having protection around her. Just a nosy musician friend who Kerrigan assured him would be made too busy to notice Cerrita's absence until it was too late. Nothing was going as planned, but Desmon was adaptable. If he couldn't grab her in this crowd, he'd follow her to the place she was currently staying.

Cerrita and DJ had their ears pressed against the door, listening in to Terrence's conversation. The insane attraction she felt for the man had withered away with each word he spoke. Cerrita had known Terrence wasn't just some Good Samaritan, but part of her had been a little flattered to think he'd followed her around like a puppy because he was attracted to her too.

Sadly, Terrence was just like all the others who'd shown interest in her, a true beast. One that could not be trusted because every last single one always had an ulterior motive. Terrence wasn't attracted to her, in fact, he thought the worst of her. He thought she was the one setting the fires, and now, he was following her as a suspect.

Worse, now DJ clearly had a lot of questions for her. "I can't believe you brought an enforcer to my shop! You know how much trouble I'll be in if he puts a single thing about my pheromone blocker in his report," she whispered.

"Sorry. I didn't know. I mean, I should have known, but I was distracted. I fucking scent marked all over him and ran out of blocker."

DJ straightened, a pained grimace on her face. "You scent marked without even..." She made a lewd thrusting gesture with her hands and pelvis.

Cerrita bit her lip and nodded.

"Well then, you are truly screwed. There usually has to be sex involved for a scent mark that strong. Being aroused shouldn't do all that, definitely not enough to need almost an entire bottle of my stuff to cover it."

"Shit. Shit. Quadruple shit!" Cerrita stalked away from the door, and DJ followed.

It was clear she was not done with her questioning, but DJ's intentions were put on hold as Terrence walked into the shop with a smile on his face like he hadn't just been talking to whoever about her being an arson suspect.

"Hi," he said casually, closing the distance between them.

The sight of Terrence in all his tall, dark, and handsome glory striding confidently to her side almost made Cerrita forget he couldn't be trusted. Her cheeks heated as he slipped a casual arm around her waist before extending his hand out to DJ.

DJ shook her head and moved around to the cash register.

"Rita filled me in on why you are here. Generic blockers are thirty dollarsfor a week's supply," DJ said with none of her usual warmth or playfulness.

Terrence didn't seem to take offense at her obvious distaste for him as he tucked his free hand into his pocket to pull out his wallet.

"How long does it take for a custom blocker like hers, and how involved is the process?" he replied.

DJ looked him up and down before sucking her teeth. "Custom orders are considered on a case by case basis. My generic blend is good for most when it comes to general use," DJ said.

"And what qualifies a special case?" Terrence pushed.

"Not you," DJ said before turning to grab a smaller black atomizer from one of the shelves behind her. "Here is a sample of my generic blocker. Test it out and only come back if you are serious about a purchase."

Terrence shoved his wallet back into his pocket and took the vial with a nod.

"If your generic blocker is half as potent as the one she has, then I'm sure I will be back," Terrence said. He glanced around the shop before adding, "I'm surprised your shop doesn't already have a line out the door with the quality of merchandise you have compared to the store downstairs."

DJ rolled her eyes. "I'm not interested in being the next IG worthy store. My customers come to me when they have real needs and are tired of wasting their money on the glorified air freshener others shill. Now, if that is all?"

Rita watched the exchange between her friend and Terrence with a mix of amusement and unease. DJ wasn't generally rude, and Terrence was an unknown factor that could bring about the end of whatever little piece of happiness Cerrita had found. She tried to focus on the fact he thought she was a suspect, and he was obviously trying to charm information from her friend, and not the way his thumb had slipped under her shirt and lightly drifted back and forth over the skin of her hip. Small movements that would seem like an absent-minded mannerism if it weren't for the way he lingered over the sensitive spot that sent her pulse racing and her swallowing hard to keep from moaning out loud. Yeah, Terrence was a master manipulator, and Cerrita would have to be extra careful not to forget why she was here with him in the first place.

"I believe she needed a refill as well. There was a bit of an accident which led us here," Terrence replied smoothly.

"Mmhm, some accident," DJ muttered, letting her eyes fall to where Terrence's hand rested on Cerrita's hip.

Cerrita was so embarrassed that if she was physically capable of blushing, her whole body would be as red as Rudolph's nose. Just shining bright like a beacon, broadcasting her misplaced horniness.

"I think I can make do with the generic blocker for now," Cerrita breathed.

"Nonsense. If you need a custom blocker, we can wait while DJ does her magic for you," Terrence said, his attention shifting to her. His brown eyes looked at her with such warmth that Cerrita was afraid she was losing control of her Phoenix fire once again.

"We?" she squeaked.

Terrence smiled at Cerrita and the combination of his pearly whites mixed with his electrifying touch had her panties wetter than a slip and slide.

"Yes. We can wait for the blocker," Terrence said before leaning over and lowering his voice to just above a whisper. "I've smelled your scent, Firefly. It's sweet and addictive and any available shifter who gets a hold of it will want to follow it to the ends of the earth. To wrap themselves up in it like a blanket, to have it coating their lips and tongue and whatever sexual organ they possess. They will try to make you theirs, and that, we both know, is a problem."

His words put Cerrita in a chokehold. The floodgates of her arousal were thrown wide open, filling the space around them with her scent. She was flushed and damn near panting at the imagery he conjured into her brain. Fuck, it should have been a turn off. She knew what it was like to be chased to the ends of the earth. It wasn't some cute little courtship tactic. It was serious and dangerous, but her brain was mush, which meant her red flag sensors were completely offline.

"My problem," she finally managed, although it came out so weak sounding as if she was unsure if it was a problem at all.

Terrence shook his head. "Not your problem, firefly. My problem. They wouldn't know it was a fool's errand to chase after what's mine."

"Yours?" Cerrita croaked.

"When you're ready, of course," Terrence said with a wink. He straightened before he turned back to DJ. "How long will it take?"

Cerrita blinked a few times before looking at her friend, who stood by shaking her head and spritzing the room with one of the generic blocker sample bottles. It was only effective in muting the pungent scent Cerrita had thrown out, not completely neutralizing it. The look DJ gave her pretty much told Cerrita all she needed to know. DJ was going to be no help at all in getting her out of this.

"I hate to say it, Rita, but he's right about you not being able to go out without your custom order. Especially, if you're going to be around him. Give me ten minutes," she said before disappearing into the back of the shop, where Cerrita knew she did all her mixing.

The shock of her one trusted friend basically abandoning her to this stranger, as well as revealing her name to him, cleared the fog of lust enough for her to separate herself from Terrence. She pushed his hand off her hip and took several steps away from him. Terrence turned to her, reaching out, but she crossed her arms over her chest and gave him her best stare down.

"I don't belong to anyone. Especially not strange men who take liberties with and make claims on women they just met," she spat.

Terrence smirked and matched her stance. "Noted, but this isn't the first time we've met, firefly. If it wasn't for that OD of Pheromone blocker you threw at us both, what you did back there was akin to a proposal. You've already put your scent on it, sweetheart, I'm just trying to honor my duties as your future mate."

"That was an accident!"

"An accident? So, you just accidentally get so aroused as to mark innocent strangers in your daily life?"

"I was agitated."

"Your denial shouldn't be so adorable." He reached out and booped her nose.

"Did you just…" The rest of the sentence died with a gasp as she was hauled into his arms.

The heat of his palms on her ass pressing her against his rock-hard body ceased all rational thought. He bent his head low, his lips brushing lightly against her cheek before he whispered, "Don't get too agitated, firefly. I don't think your friend will appreciate it if she has to use up all her stock to cover the aftermath."

"Aftermath?"

"Ever heard of the expression a dog with a scent?"

Cerrita shook her head. She wasn't even sure what her own name was. All she knew was she wanted him closer. She wrapped her arms around his neck, keeping him at eye level with her.

"A dog with a scent is relentless in his pursuit. He'll track it to the ends of the earth, and once it's found, if the scent is a real good one, he'll roll all over it, letting it seep into his fur and cling to his skin."

"What does that have to do with this?"

"Everything, firefly. I'm a Hellhound, and I've caught your scent. Release it again, and I'll have no choice. I'll be all over you."

The image he conjured both confused and aroused Cerrita. The urge to swoon was great,, but she bit the inside of her cheek to snap herself back to reality.

"That sounds awful," Cerrita lied.

Terrence looked stricken by her words and tried to stand, but her arms were still locked tight around his neck. He gently pried her hands from around his neck.

"On that note, I should probably go."

Cerrita bit her lip and took a step back. Her words had effectively cut the sexual tension between them, but the sudden chill emanating from him made Cerrita second guess just how safe she was around Terrence Shaw.

"You got what you came here for. Nothing stopping you from going about your day," Cerrita doubled down.

Terrence studied her for a minute before she saw when he made the decision to leave. His shoulders tensed up and he ran a hand over his short cropped hair before reaching into his pocket and pulling out a small white business card.

He offered it to her, but when she didn't reach for it, he tossed it on the counter next to her.

"No, firefly, I didn't, but I'm not an asshole. I'll respect your wish for me to go. Don't leave until you have the blocker from DJ, and there's my card. If you need help with anything, hit me up." With that, he turned and marched out of the store.

Terrence leaned against the wall outside the door to Rita's friend's shop. Rita, the name, her name, was just as short and spicy as the woman it belonged to. He had half a mind to march back inside and show her just how much she affected him. Just how wrong she was about whatever kept her at arm's length. The anger building inside him wasn't safe for the general public. Managing your emotions was skill level one for Hellhound shifters. The tendency toward violence in them was strong. One of the reasons Hellhounds sought out more violent careers as fighters or more legally as enforcers. Hellhounds were the ultimate killing machines. They could easily rip humans and other beasts to shreds. The added ability to drag people and creatures to Hell was a bit of overkill. It was highly recommended to stay on the good side of a Hellhound.

He hoped Rita knew his anger wasn't toward her. It was at whoever had caused the hurt he'd seen in her eyes. The deep kind that caused people to mistrust even the air they breathed for fear of experiencing that kind of pain again. Her words hurt, too. His ego was definitely bruised, but this anger he felt was something else. He'd trained his entire life to manage his emotions. To think clearly no matter the situation, and yet here he was nearly hyperventilating with rage because of one woman's fear-based rejection.

Whoever had hurt Rita was now top on Terrence's shit list, but finding out who that person was had to wait. He had a case to solve, and he needed to get his shit together before he put himself and his career at greater risk. All for a woman who couldn't even admit to the crazy attraction between them. Pushing off the wall, Terrence pulled out his phone and dialed Harvey back.

"You done getting your dick wet?" Harvey answered.

"Fuck off, Harv. What's going on with this new fire?" Terrence bit out. He was not in the mood for his brother's childish behavior and immediately regretted dialing Harvey instead of Sampson.

"Definitely Phoenix fire, but this one differs from the others. There's no obvious target, no important players can be connected to the land or anything. The others were clearly deliberate, but this one feels different. It was smaller, not as strategic to ruffle feathers. Not to mention, it's about as far as it can be from your location downtown."

That didn't sound good. He was sure Rita couldn't possibly be the culprit, but the new details were not looking good for her.

"You think it was set to be a distraction?" He shoved his free hand into his pocket to keep from punching something.

"Can't say definitively, but why don't you tell me about your little distraction at the market?" Harvey said.

Terrence sighed heavily. "I'm not in a secure enough location to discuss that. Send a couple beats to the market, and I'll meet you at HQ."

He didn't give Harvey a chance to reply before he ended the call. With one last glance toward the shop entrance, Terrence headed down the stairs. There should already be a few low-level enforcers nearby the market, and he wanted to make sure they all knew who to look out for before he'd feel even remotely comfortable leaving Rita's side.

Two enforcers messaged that they were at the market before he made it completely down the stairs. He met them at the front of the larger store and gave them a quick rundown on what to look out for and when to contact him before he cut out to meet up with his brother. He hoped once they put the pieces together with this new fire, they could not only exonerate Rita, but get a bead on the actual arsonist.

Leaving Rita behind without a guarantee he would see her again was a pain, especially with how his Hellhound protested. It snarled and thrashed around in a fit of frustration and rage like Terrence had never experienced. This level of attraction was dangerous indeed. Both he and his Hellhound needed to put space between them and Rita before they ended up doing something they would both regret.

A Low Blow

"Let me walk you out," DJ offered when Cerrita finished telling her what happened with Terrence while she was in the back mixing up the blocker for her.

"I'll be fine. He's probably long gone by now."

"Girl, I am not worried about that man! I'm actually a little mad you didn't jump his fine ass. Don't forget his card, by the way."

"Wait, what?"

DJ rolled her eyes and shoved the card into Cerrita's hand. "You came in this morning worried about your ex having found you, and then we find out you're a suspect in a high-profile arson investigation. From what you told me about your ex, he could be framing your ass so you don't have a choice but to go back to him and your old life for protection. I'd feel much better if Mr. Shaw had stayed with you."

Cerrita didn't want to admit to DJ that she knew that was what Desmon was doing. It wasn't the first time he'd done it either, just never in a town big enough to garner this much attention.

"Maybe, or none of this has anything to do with me and I'm just being paranoid."

"Doubtful. Let me grab my purse, and I will walk you to your car. Maybe you should call off of work for the day. Stay home until this situation blows over," DJ said.

"Fine, you can walk me to my car, but that's it, DJ. I ran so I could live my life how I saw fit. If he is behind all of this, I refuse to let him chase me back into a cage. That's why I need your help finding out more information about Phoenix," Cerrita said.

"I get it, but you also need to be safe out there. Like Mr. Shaw so adequately put, if you get too overwhelmed and scent bomb in public again, your ex won't be the only one you need to run from," DJ warned before disappearing into the back again to grab her things.

The two women were mostly silent as they made their way across the market. It was late afternoon, and the crowds had dwindled to a handful of people. The lack of traffic made spotting the two enforcers trailing them much easier. Cerrita didn't acknowledge them but was grateful when it appeared they wouldn't be following her home, at least. Neither made a move to get a vehicle when she pulled away, leaving DJ standing at the curb waving her off.

Still, Cerrita couldn't shake the feeling of being watched, of being hunted. She ducked her head to get a better look at the sky above her car and cursed as she saw the faint shadow of a large bird in the clouds above.

"Fucking Desmon."

Tossing the case file from the previous fire aside, Terrence looked up to find his two brothers staring back at him. Born the same day but hours apart, one would think they would be somewhat similar but the three of them couldn't be any different. Sampson was technically the oldest, and he loved to pull the rank card whenever it suited him to be the man in charge. Some would call him stoic. Harvey and Terrence just called him a boring stick in the mud. Harvey was the youngest in their trio and acted like it. He was a prankster and loved pissing people off just for the sake of starting shit. Ever the adrenaline junky, Terrence could tell the thrill of fighting fires, more specifically Phoenix fires, could easily become an obsession for him.

Terrence was right in the middle; both in time of birth and general temperament. He could crack a joke and be the life of the party one night, and the next, kick everyone out so he could lounge in his favorite chair with a glass of cognac and the latest issue of Supernatural Science Weekly. Although, at the moment, he was spite reading through a series of Gen Ursa novels. For that, he could blame Edi. Their sister had left her prized collection of romance novels in his care while she enjoyed her new promotion in Hell.

"You got any insights or are you just going to sit there glaring at us?" Sampson said after a moment.

Terrence shifted in his chair. "Rita is definitely connected, but I still don't think she is the one setting the fires."

"That your professional opinion or your dick's?" Harvey asked.

If Terrence was being honest with himself, he had no clue. Rita had definitely caught him off-guard. Something that should never happen, especially during an investigation. Now, he was questioning his gut. How could he possibly separate his burning desire to protect her in this situation? Of course, he couldn't tell Harvey that.

"How about you focus more on this case and less on my dick, you bastard?"

"Focus, children," Sampson snapped at them both before Harvey could say whatever crazy shit he had lined up to say next. "Terrence, answer the question. Is this Rita a conflict of interest for you?"

Terrence sighed. He wanted to say no, but that would be a lie. Saying yes would also be a lie because no matter how he felt, if Rita was serious about not really wanting him, he would respect that. It wasn't his place to question or push for what she'd already said no to.

"Maybe. Regardless, I handed her over to the beats, so I can focus on other leads."

"Do we even have any other leads right now?" Harvey sighed.

Terrence sat back and went over the case details in his head. So far, there have been three fires. The first two had been smaller structural fires. The damage there had been limited to some burnt up paperwork and some smoke and water damage. The first at an accounting firm that handled the books of a few of the mafia heads in the area. The second was a known human mafia warehouse. Nothing kept there would be of any major importance. It would all be expendable things that wouldn't make a dent in their operations when the cops did their monthly raid.

That was why they had originally assumed it was some human mafia beef, as it wasn't uncommon for Supernaturals to end up in their lower ranks. One could have easily used their connections and abilities to start the fires on behalf of their employer. The third fire at the Pack leader's mansion, however, had tipped the scales.

The mafia and the Pack had a longstanding truce, mostly because the humans knew their limits and facing off with a bunch of magical and shapeshifting creatures wasn't a risk worth taking. Even if it seemed the Pack was making a move against them, they wouldn't be dumb enough to attack the Pack head directly. Which meant, there was another player, someone who stood to gain from there being discord between the two parties. That only left one person, the only person they couldn't touch. Kevin Kerrigan.

The slimy bastard was a prince of Hell, and thus, way above their pay grade to bring down. The world worked with a precarious balance. Kevin Kerrigan was the lesser of the evils that could be left to run amuck in the human realm. Still a dangerous daemon spawn, but his ambitions were less about violence and more about obtaining power. These very loud, very public fires weren't his MO, at least, not for the long game. That would require bringing both the mafia and the Pack structure to their knees.

"Rock, paper, scissors on who gets to pay our neighborhood daemon lord a visit," Terrence said.

Both Sampson and Harvey groaned aloud.

"I was really hoping to avoid tying this shit to him," Sampson said.

"Rock, paper, scissors, my ass! You two get to it. I'm banned from all interaction with that motherfucker after the last incident," Harvey said.

"Lucky punk," Sampson muttered, readying his hands for the exchange.

Terrence scooted forward and balled up one fist before laying the other flat in front of his brother's.

"Rock, paper, scissors, shoot," they chanted.

Round one, they both picked rock.

"Rock, paper, scissors, shoot."

Round two, they both picked scissors.

"Rock, paper, scissors, shoot!"

This time, Sampson picked rock again, but Terrence had somehow mixed up his signs in his indecision and landed with his middle finger out for scissors and the rest of his hand in a fist for rock. Harvey burst out laughing and Sampson knocked Terrence's hand away.

"I don't have time for this childish bullshit! Terrence has to go to Club Hellfire tonight to chat up the waitresses for info, anyway, since he's the only one not banned from those premises," Sampson said.

Terrence had almost forgotten about Elias Westmoore and his not-so-subtle hint about finding a Phoenix in Mulberry.

"Does he really, though? I mean, he found one already. The odds of there being a second rogue Phoenix in the area is pretty fucking small," Harvey said.

What were the odds of there being two Phoenixes in Mulberry without anyone's knowledge? Slim to fucking none, but that was Terrence's working theory. It had to be the case, otherwise, he'd know he was compromised. If Rita was the culprit, he'd be devastated. Not only because he'd have to drag her pretty ass to Hell, but she'd be taking him with her.

Fuck, was he really that hung up over some strange girl he was willing to suffer Hell for eternity just to be by her side? That settled it, he was losing his mind. He wouldn't just go to Club Hellfire that evening to gather intel. He'd be sure to pick up a willing partner to distract him from Rita, and maybe that would get him back on track. Maybe then he could break whatever spell her scent had cast upon him, and he'd be free to close this case without also closing the book on his career as an enforcer.

"We don't know for sure his hint was about the Phoenix. He could be hinting at someone suspicious, who'd want to hurt the Pack besides the obvious suspects," Terrence rationalized.

Both of his brothers eyed him suspiciously.

"You have a point. Like the tip of a needle, maybe less, but still a valid point," Sampson said.

"Then, it's settled. Sampson's going to visit the daemon spawn, I'll hit up the staff at Club Hellfire, and Harvey can pull the overnight shift at the office and finally make that overpriced chemistry set work for us, instead of just being a useless pile of junk taking up prime real estate.

"Give me some fucking evidence I can work with and watch that 'pile of junk' more than pay for itself," Harvey scoffed.

Terrence pulled the generic blocker he'd gotten from Jourdain Alchemy from his pocket.

"I'm pretty sure this blocker is what's holding up half the cases in our unsolved pile. I got you a full bottle to analyze this time. Make yourself useful and figure that shit out."

Harvey took the vial, a glimmer of excitement in his eyes as he studied it. They may rag on Harvey for being an immature prick, but the boy had some brains on him. If DJ's special formula was to blame for running their closed case record into the ground, he'd surely figure it out in no time.

With Harvey distracted and Sampson already having disappeared into his private office, Terrence grabbed his keys and headed for the door. He needed to shower and change into something more suitable for the evening. Something that didn't scream "on duty enforcer". Of course, they would already know who he was, but as long as he was just there for fun, he wouldn't ruffle too many feathers with his appearance at one of the shadiest clubs in town.

Kevin Kerrigan may be a daemon prince, but Koda was *the* daemon prince, the heir apparent to the throne of Hell and owner of Club Hellfire. He didn't abide by anyone's bullshit, and once inside, he was subject to the rules and laws of Hell, which were basically don't start shit you can't back up with your fists. He was treading a dangerous line tonight, but one he had to tread fairly often.

Technically, he was a subject of Hell as a Hellhound, which meant he was welcome as long as he kept his alliance with the Mulberry Pack checked at the door. The staff there would know of any newcomers who seemed a bit off. Whether or not they would talk was another story.

A Real Piece of Work

The last place most women would be was work when they knew their stalker ex had found them, but Cerrita knew for her it was the safest place to be right now. Earlier that day she regretted switching shifts, but not now. As long as she was on duty, Cerrita knew she had a few guaranteed hours of peace. Desmon couldn't touch her here. Although, Cerrita couldn't guarantee she was completely safe within the walls of the club.

Night shift at Club Hellfire was completely new to Cerrita. Not only was the crowd a lot rowdier, but the night shift uniform left very little to the imagination. Even in the most modest version of the outfit, the high waist of the shorts was only a small consolation considering the bottom of them were cut high, exposing over half her ass cheeks to the handsy patrons. The options for tops were even more revealing. A shimmery stretch tube that was just wide enough to hide one's nipples, or the "covered" version which was a neon-colored fishnet top with a white triangle bikini top underneath.

The worst part of the outfit was the 4-inch strappy sandals she wore on her feet. During the day, they were allowed to wear tennis shoes, but apparently night shift was a special kind of torture. Running drinks through a crowded club was hard enough. Adding being on stilts to the equation and Cerrita's calves were cramping within ten minutes of being on the floor.

"Move out the way, new girl. You gotta work fast to get the big tips," one of the night shift waitresses said, leaning past Cerrita to finish garnishing the drinks on her tray.

"Leave Rita alone, Mila. She's only here tonight as a favor to your bestie," Fancy snapped.

Mila rolled her eyes but didn't say anything more to Cerrita.

"Thanks," Cerrita thanked Fancy.

"Don't thank me, just pick up the pace. Slow drinks mean a grumpy crowd, and we don't want our patrons to have any reason to have a worse attitude," Fancy said.

"Right," Cerrita breathed and grabbed her tray.

Cerrita had only seen a fight at Hellfire one time during the day shift and had been appalled at the ruthless violence displayed. She'd nearly laughed it off when Fancy said it was child's play compared to some of the fights that happened during night shift. Cerrita wasn't willing to be the cause, directly or indirectly, of any fight, so despite her tight calves and aching feet, she sauntered back into the crowd. Her section was small and closer to the VIP section. That meant she wasn't as on demand as the other waitresses but still had plenty to keep her busy going back and forth between the bar and the patrons.

How the other waitresses dealt with the weird energy that permeated the space, Cerrita didn't know. On one hand, there were plenty of people on the dance floor, letting go to the thumping beats of the latest hip hop. Their energy felt playful and infectious. At the tables and the VIP section was a more serious energy. Cerrita wasn't naïve to what went down in the VIP area. It was the worst kept secret that the most powerful and dangerous Supernaturals in Mulberry frequented VIP to make deals, form alliances, and plan all sorts of business ventures, as well as nefarious activities.

The sense of foreboding almost overwhelmed her each time she made her rounds on the tables closest to the VIP. The patrons there were mostly security and high-level goons that hadn't quite made the cut when it came to listening in to the dealings. Cerrita moved faster to make sure those patrons were well served.

After her tenth trip to the bar, Cerrita hazarded a glance at a nearby phone to check the time. Was it really only one a.m.? Time seemed to fly and crawl all at once. Her shift wouldn't be over until three. Two more hours, and then she would have to worry about what Desmon's next steps were. He'd left her alone for the few hours before her shift. That was progress, at least. In the past, he'd wasted no time in trying to snatch her up as soon as she was in his sights.

Maybe this time he wanted her to come to him. If that was the case, he could die waiting. She was so over his bullshit and would no longer allow herself to be a victim of his manipulations. Either way, she was looking at a sleepless morning.

The mental exhaustion of having to fend off Mr. Grab Hands every time she served his table wasn't helping the fatigue she felt about her current situation. She wasn't about to complain about this well-paying job with flexible hours, but Cerrita was definitely not going to take anymore night shifts, no matter how much more the night shift girls made. The accepted amount of harassment was too much for her, even as the other girls seemed to thrive on the attention.

Part of Cerrita was ready to just call it quits for the night, especially when a patron palmed her ass as she walked by. It took everything in Cerrita to just walk away, ignoring the Grab Hands and avoiding eye contact, so as not to encourage more unwanted interactions. The last thing she needed was to go off on a customer and lose her job altogether. Tired or not, she could make it through this shift. She'd just be extra careful to dodge Grab Hands.

She had only managed a few steps before the man grabbed her arm. "Hey! Where are you going?"

Cerrita tugged her arm away. "To do my job."

She started to walk away again but Grab Hands moved around her, cutting her off from her planned escape route. She tried to move around him and find another way through the crowd, but it seemed his buddies were backing him up. For each move she made, they boxed her in closer to Grab Hands. Cerrita gripped her tray tighter, ready to use it as a shield if she needed to push through the men in front of her. With a sigh, Cerrita finally looked Grab hands in the eye, mustering her best customer service smile.

"Sir, I know you are aware that harassment of an employee of Koda will not be tolerated." Cerrita regurgitated the script she'd memorized during her training. While she had no idea what the consequences were exactly, just the utterance of the club owner's name generally had people running the other direction. Cerrita hadn't met him personally. Fancy was the bar manager and handled everything as far as she could tell. However, this man was either new to the area or too drunk to care.

As this was the fourth bottle Cerrita had delivered to the table, it was certainly the latter. That made this situation all the more dangerous. Cerrita once again tried to peer around the man, to signal one of the other waitresses or better yet Fancy, but she was a little too short even in the stilts masquerading as footwear she currently wore.

"Is there a problem here?" A familiar voice rose above the club music.

Grab Hands looked over his shoulder, a cocky grin on his face as he fixed his mouth to say something smart. Only when his eyes met the darkness at his back, he visibly recoiled and began to stammer, "Uh no, no problem at all."

"Good to hear. I hope you are tipping this lovely woman graciously for putting up with your inappropriate antics," Terrence continued.

Grab Hands nodded enthusiastically before digging out his wallet and dropping every dollar in the fold onto Cerrita's tray. Upon seeing Terrence emerge from the crowd as if he'd been hiding there all along in the shadows, Cerrita dropped her gaze to her tray.

What the fuck was he doing here?

Apparently, Desmon wasn't the only man stalking her. She couldn't for the life of her feel as put out about it as she should be. Cerrita did her best to keep her face neutral as she counted just how many hundreds were now on her tray. When she did look up, though, Grab Hands and his goons were gone, and so was Terrence. The man seemed to be made of shadows because for the life of her Cerrita couldn't recall the man making an entrance that wasn't like a rabbit being pulled from a hat. How he got there and why he suddenly appeared was always a mystery. Yet, her body was left with a tingling akin to a level of excitement she had never experienced before.

Shaking her head, Cerrita grabbed the bills before anyone else grabbed them off her tray and headed straight for the bar. Fancy stood behind the bar with their arms folded over their chest looking directly at Cerrita. The expression on their face showed displeasure and Cerrita had a feeling she wasn't going to like the ass chewing she got from her boss. Cerrita set her tray down and started to count and split the massive tip when Fancy covered her hand.

"Keep it, you're done for the night."

Cerrita stopped counting the money and frowned. "Did I do something wrong?"

Fancy breathed out a rough sigh. "Look, most of the girls here have got some kinda story and as long as it doesn't interfere with business here, I don't get involved. However, you know the rules. No significant others allowed while you are on shift. Since this is your first offense, you're off the floor for retraining."

Cerrita became even more confused. "What? I think you have the wrong idea. I'm not seeing anyone."

Fancy cocked their head to the side, showing that they didn't believe Cerrita.

"Take the money. It should tide you over until you are cleared to work again."

"I'm not lying," Rita protested.

"Maybe not about the boyfriend shit, but if more than one enforcer shows up with a special interest in you, that ain't good for business either. An active investigation anywhere near this place will run this place dry."

Cerrita's scowl deepened. She hadn't known Terrence was there until he revealed himself, and yet, she had seen the two enforcers who'd followed her at the market at the beginning of her shift.

"I'm sure it's just a misunderstanding," Cerrita said.

"Doesn't change a thing, sweetheart. Go home, get some rest, and maybe figure out why you are being targeted. The sooner this is cleared up the better," Fancy said and went back to bartending.

Cerrita tucked the money into her top and marched off toward the changing room. Terrence Shaw was becoming an issue. Cerrita had enough problems with Desmon. Now she had to figure out how to shake a Hellhound enforcer as well. Two impossible feats, one determined Phoenix.

Only Time Will Tell

Terrence leaned against his SUV and watched the men he'd escorted out of Club Hellfire climb into their vehicles and pull off. His eyes tracked them until they were out of sight. So much for getting inside information from the waitresses. They hadn't been forthcoming with any information pertinent to the case.

On the other hand, he'd run into Rita again. It shouldn't have been a surprise if the beats he'd left in charge of watching her had done their job correctly. Not only had they not notified him of her location, but neither had been at the club when he'd arrived. Both things were unacceptable, and they would surely hear about it later, but for now, he focused on the positives. He'd peeled another layer of her mystery and his case. The men he'd just run off worked for Kevin Kerrigan. The standard issue goon suits they wore along with the air of untouchable had been a dead giveaway. Their leader with the grabby hands had been trying to catch Rita's scent all night. A surefire way for him to track her down later, outside of the protection of the club. Terrence pulled out his phone and texted his brothers.

T: Bro, any luck with the daemon spawn?

S: What do you think?

T: His men were checking out my Phoenix suspect.

S: Confirms she's involved in this somehow. We just need to find out why she would be important enough for Kevin to stick his neck out like this.

H: He's a textbook narcissist. He wants ultimate power and having a Phoenix around would give him that.

S: True, but he's being cautious about it. There is something else going on here.

T: On it. I'll escort her home. See if she opens up after I tell her the danger she's in.

H: You need back up?

S: I can be there in five

T: No, I've got her. Don't want to bring the whole might of the Hellhounds on a possible innocent.

S: Don't underestimate the suspect. Especially, if she is a Phoenix.

T: I'm not stupid. She just doesn't seem like the criminal arsonist type.

H: And what type does she seem like?

T: The innocent type

S: Still think she's innocent in all of this?

T: I know it doesn't look good given the information we have, but I have to go with my gut on this.

S: Right. Just remember that she is STILL A SUSPECT and treat her as such.

T: I won't forget.

H: You sure you don't need backup? Sounds like maybe Sampson or I should take over watching the Phoenix.

Terrence didn't like the idea of leaving Rita in the hands of his brothers. Hell, he hated the idea of leaving her with anyone but him, but that was a discussion he needed to have with himself later. Right now, he was doing his best to manage his possessive feelings for Rita and focus on closing the case.

T: I've got this. You find anything with the blocker I gave you?

H: Not yet, but mind sharing where you got this stuff. It's potent as shit. Definitely what was used in some of the crimes so far, but no luck in sorting through the scents to find the smoking gun.

Terrence was saved from answering when Rita came breezing out the front door. He frowned. No employee left out the front like that, especially during business hours and still in uniform. Not only that, but she was limping. He shoved his phone in his pocket and rushed to her side.

Desmon circled the parking lot once more, watching as the enforcer chased off more of Kerrigan's men. Men Desmon hadn't ordered. He knew he shouldn't have trusted Kerrigan not to go after Rita himself. Never trust a daemon, even half of one.

This enforcer was going to be more of a nuisance than Desmon originally thought. He'd heard what the enforcer had sneered at Kerrigan's men. He'd had the gall to claim Cerrita as his own.

Not on Desmon's watch. He'd come too far to allow this beast to swoop in and claim what was rightfully his. He knew the beast's claims were false. Cerrita would never lay with such an animal. She might feel angry about his deception, but she knew who she belonged to.

Who her body needed to unlock her true power. She wouldn't defile herself with anyone else. If she did? Well, that didn't matter so much. He could still take her power as his own whether she was willing or not. Would it be easier if she ruled by his side, sure.

Two Phoenixes in a united front would ensure no one got ideas about challenging him, but he could wield both of their magic on his own just as easily. Those who thought they could best him once he came to full power would quickly learn the error of their ways. Desmon had already started a mental list of those he'd make bow before him once his plans were realized. Watching the way the enforcer fawned over Cerrita earned the man a spot on that list, right under Kevin Kerrigan's duplicitous ass.

This would be the last time Desmon chased after Cerrita. He was done playing games. She would yield to him or watch as he stole her power from her.

Cerrita looked up to the sky, not surprised to see Desmon's silhouette circling the parking lot. He hadn't yet made his move, but he was making it clear he was watching. She hefted her bag on her shoulder and took a step toward her car.

Both feet were sore from hours in heels, but her left foot ached extra because of the clumsy asshole who smashed her toes as she'd tried to make a dignified march to the employee locker room to get her stuff. As much as she would have loved to slip on her much more comfortable tennis shoes, she was afraid of how much her feet would hurt once she slipped off the strappy torture boots she wore.

No, taking them off would have to wait until she could get home and soak them in an Epsom salt bath. For now, she just had to make it to her car. The universe had other plans as her gaze dropped from the sky and fell right on Terrence jogging over to her. The last person she wanted to see, especially after he just got her suspended. Rita didn't want to run any longer, but he'd just made that a harder choice for her to make. Without the tips from being on the floor, she would run low on funds quickly with the expense of the city. He'd unwittingly ripped the rug out from under her.

"Are you okay?" he asked.

Rita glared up at him and rolled her eyes. "Get away from me," she huffed and hobbled forward.

She had only managed a few steps before the weight of her duffle combined with the stilts she wore knocked her off balance. She pitched to the side; he caught her in his arms before she hit the ground.

"Let me just help you to your car."

"You've helped enough," she grumbled, even as she allowed him to slip the bag from her shoulder and hook an arm around her waist. She leaned into him to steady herself, but when it came time to let go, she found herself leaning closer.

His arms holding her up relieved some of the pressure off her aching feet and then there was the zip of electric arousal that ran through her whenever he was this close. Terrence Shaw was dangerous, not just because of his job but because he seemed destined to destroy her. The thought should have given her the swift kick in the rear to push away. To stand on her own two feet and make it clear his help wasn't something she would ever want or need.

Yet, one tentative step had her leaning even more on him. She had been right about the pressure keeping her feet from exploding in pain. What he thought was help had only done exactly what she had hoped to avoid. She glanced to where her car was parked, and it seemed infinitely farther than it had just a moment ago.

"Fine, you can help me to my car, but after that, I never want to see you again," she huffed.

"Fair enough," Terrence muttered, but instead of just letting her lean on him and hobble, he swept her into his arms, cradling her against his chest.

"What are you doing?"

"Helping you to your car."

"I can still walk," she protested.

"Maybe, but if this is the last chance I have to hold you in my arms, I'm going to take it."

"Fuck! This is why I don't have a job right now. Stupid men just deciding things about me and my life and ruining any chance I have of being happy and independent."

Terrence froze and looked down at her. "What men?" he growled.

Cerrita chewed the inside of her cheek. She hadn't meant to reveal anything more to Terrence about her life, but once again, she was finding her brain just didn't work properly when around this man. He was a distraction she didn't need. A distraction she couldn't afford. Glancing up at the sky, she saw Desmon hovering above.

Maybe she had a chance to salvage this situation once and for all. She wrapped her arms around Terrence's neck and leaned in just shy of their lips touching. "Men like you. Men who see me as an object to possess. A shiny trophy to add to their collection. A vessel for all their power mad desires."

"Firefly, if that's what you think, I definitely have my work cut out for me. I don't want to control you. I want you to be happy and independent and whatever else you want to be. The only thing I want is to know you're safe and well loved by me."

Cerrita tossed her head back and laughed.

"Cut the crap and put me down. I've got enough shit to deal with."

She wiggled in his grasp, but Terrence held tight until he deposited her in front of her car.

"You're upset. Drive home safe, and don't forget to call me when you figure out I'm not your enemy here."

With that, he handed her back her duffle bag and marched off to his own vehicle. She watched him as he climbed into his SUV before she climbed into her car. Tossing her duffle into the back seat, she checked the skies again before she pulled off. She no longer saw Desmon hovering above, but that didn't mean he wasn't there.

She pulled away from the curb and took the long back and forth route she used in case someone attempted to follow her home. It wasn't until she stopped feeling like she was being watched that she finally took her tired aching self home.

First thing she'd do when she got home was take off those damn shoes, then she would run a nice hot bath to soak away the stress of the day. Then she would spend the rest of the night scouring the internet for any snatch of information that could help her with getting Desmon off her back for good. It wasn't like she would be getting any sleep that night anyway.

Her home should have been dark when she arrived. Aside from the small light on the front porch, all the lights inside should have been off. Not exactly the safest, but Cerrita wasn't in any position to play fast and loose about her light bill, even before getting fired. The flickering light of flames dancing in the front window was enough evidence that someone had gotten into her home, the second was the fact that her door wasn't closed. Smoke poured from inside her home.

Her heart raced in her chest. Desmon knew where she lived, and this was his housewarming gift. He was making his move. Apparently, fake canoodling with Terrence had been a mistake. With no other option, she pulled away from her house and drove around the block before pulling over again to pull out her phone. She tried calling DJ, but her phone went straight to voicemail twice. For a moment, Cerrita contemplated heading downtown to catch DJ at Hotel K, but that was just as dangerous as walking into her burning home where Desmon probably waited for her. She felt the familiar tingle of panic spread through her body.

Calm down. Calm down. We're okay. Calm down.

She chanted to herself as she wrestled her emotions back into the tiny space she kept them shoved away. She needed to make a clear and rational decision about this. She didn't have enough on her to make a run for it. Well, she did, but she didn't want to leave her Phoenix tome behind. She knew it had the answers she was looking for in it somewhere, but she would never find it if she allowed Desmon to make her leave it behind.

With a curse, Cerrita knew what she needed to do, and she really didn't want to do it. She reached into her purse and pulled out the small white card Terrence had left behind. Picking up her phone, she dialed his number. He answered on the first ring.

"I'm right behind you. Get out of your car and get in the SUV parked three cars back," he said.

"I should have known you followed me."

"To the ends of the earth. I told you, firefly, I've got your scent."

"We'll discuss your creepy behavior when I'm not in danger," she replied before grabbing her things and abandoning her car in search of Terrence's.

After Rita hung up, Terrence got out of the SUV to meet her because his beast wouldn't calm its shit until she was safely in his arms. She was also probably still limping in those sexy as fuck heels she wore. Part of him was happy he was right about Rita being a victim in all of this. The other wanted to rip whoever was after her to shreds.

The guys at the club had belonged to Kevin Kerrigan, but under no circumstances would Kevin want to hurt a potential asset. No, this fire had been set to send a message. A message that Rita wasn't untouchable, but Terrence didn't know who the message was for. Did this fire have anything to do with the others? He was still missing something big in all of this.

Something he hoped Rita was ready to share with him. His long strides made the three-car distance between him and Rita in no time. She was bent over trying to tug her duffle bag out of the back seat but only managed to give him a taste of what she would look like while being fucked from behind, the delicate curvature of her ass cheeks on full display, rocking back and forth, flexing and contracting. Terrence adjusted himself before clearing his throat. "Need some help, firefly?"

She yelped and scrambled out of the car; her injured foot apparently forgotten because as soon as she put weight on it, she toppled forward, right into his arms.

"You! You beast!" She muttered, trying to push out of his arms, but he held her tight against him while he reached into her car and grabbed her bag with no issue.

"Your beast. I'm your beast, and I'm here to save your sweet ass, so do me a favor and hold on tight," Terrence said.

She cocked her head to the side, no doubt ready to give him an earful, but he bent down and lifted her up, his arm under her ass, and he carried her like a small child to his car.

"I can't believe this shit," she hissed, clinging to his neck.

"Not a fan of twisted fairy tales I presume?" Terrence teased as he settled her into the passenger side of his SUV and buckled her in. She pressed her lips together, but Terrence didn't miss the shaky quality of her breath as his arm brushed her thigh.

"Can you just drop me at this address? I can find my way from there," she said, holding up her phone.

Terrence scowled when he recognized the address for Hotel K. Maybe his little firefly wasn't so innocent after all.

"Not in this life, or the next. I'm taking you somewhere safe, and then you and I are going to have a nice little chat about what the fuck is going on," Terrence said and shut the door.

He jogged around to the driver's side and climbed in.

"There is nothing to discuss," Rita said as soon as he was in the car.

"Oh, there will be, once my brothers get back to me with the arson report for your home."

Her eyes grew wide at his words, and he smirked before pulling off in the direction of his home. Should he have taken her to the enforcer office? Fuck yes. But he knew that would only clam her up more. She needed to be comfortable if he had any chance of getting her to open up, and the selfish part of him urged him to get her alone and near a bed to do it. Protocol be damned.

Dark Night of the Soul

As soon as Terrence pulled up to the red brick brownstone, Cerita dropped a pin on the location for DJ. She'd fully expected him to bring her to the enforcer office or even Pack headquarters, but with the way he'd kept his hand on her thigh the whole ride, she should have been prepared for him to take her to his home.

"Are you serious right now?" she asked him as he helped her out of the SUV.

"Until I know what's going on, this is the safest place for us to have the conversation we need to have," he said.

"Again, there is no conversation to be had," she sighed.

Terence shouldered her duffle before picking her up again. She didn't even bother protesting at this point. Her feet throbbed, and she was almost sure one was broken at this point. To be honest with herself, she also enjoyed the feel of being in his arms more than she cared to admit. It took every ounce of willpower not to snuggle into him, or suck his earlobe into her mouth, or nibble on his strong muscle-corded neck.

Maybe she really did need to take DJ's advice. Terrence couldn't possibly want to talk if he was balls deep in her vagina. She'd get off without having to talk and he'd just get off. It was a win-win.

"What are you thinking about, firefly?" he groaned.

"Oh nothing," she sighed, settling her head on his shoulder.

"Really, because my arm is feeling a little wet, and your scent..." He paused to take a deep breath before releasing it with a moan.

"Don't think for a second I am above fucking the answers I need out of you," he finished as he swung the front door open.

Cerrita wiggled in his arms and nipped at his earlobe. "I'd like to see you try."

Terrence flicked on a light, bathing the small living room space with a soft warm glow, before kicking the door shut and carrying her to a black leather couch. He set her down gently before moving to the small open concept kitchen on the other side of the room.

"I'll get some ice for your foot," he grumbled.

Cerrita watched with amusement as he fumbled around his own kitchen. First, grabbing a box of plastic bags from a drawer before taking an ice cube tray out of the freezer. He muttered to himself while he placed ice in a bag, one cube at a time. He was obviously stalling and giving himself a pep talk at the same time.

While he was distracted, Cerrita took the time to study his space. She didn't really know Terrence, but the decor of his home seemed to fit him. The space might be decent, but his oversized furniture made it look miniscule. She snorted with laughter at the thought of herself as Jack exploring the giant of the beanstalk's castle. Huge furniture, exposed brick walls, and a fireplace mantel lined with leather-bound books.

Everything looked like him, except for the book on the dark wood coffee.

"Your girlfriend left this behind?" she said, holding up the well-read romance novel.

Terrence's gaze shot up and his eyes narrowed. "Are you jealous?"

Cerrita shook her head, even if he was right on the mark with how she felt. "Not in the least," she lied.

"You know what I am, who I am. You really think an obvious lie like that will work on me?" He finished with the ice and wrapped a towel around the bag before joining her on the couch. He lifted her foot into his lap and undid the straps on her shoes.

She winced as he pried the first shoe from her swollen feet. It wasn't even the injured one. His thick fingers wrapped around her ankle, sending a jolt of awareness through her body so sharp she sank deeper into the couch, allowing him to bring both of her feet into his lap.

"That's it, love, just relax. I'm going to take off your other shoe now. It's going to hurt, but don't worry. I promise to make it all better." His tone was soft but laced with desire and promise.

He carefully eased the heel away much slower than he had the first. It hurt, but he took his time. With each painful strap he removed, he took the time to massage the pain away, and when the shoe was gone, he carefully inspected her foot.

"Good news is, I don't think your whole foot is broken, just one or two of your toes. Nothing a shift can't fix."

At the word shift, Cerrita sat up. "No, no shifting."

Terrence only nodded and continued to massage her foot, working from the heel up but skipping her injured toes. The feel of his large, warm hands kneading her flesh had her reclining further into the couch as waves of arousal coursed through her body. Then he switched to her other foot, working out the tension in those toes until she hummed with pleasure.

"Ugh, who needs sex with foot rubs like this?" she breathed. Her panties were soaked, her core was throbbing, and all it would take was the press of a finger, or hell, a stiff breeze to send her over the edge, and all because he'd been the one giving it to her.

"You haven't had sex with me yet. That is the only reason you would utter such a blasphemous statement," Terrence chuckled.

"Mmm, I mean, I wouldn't know the difference, anyway. My only experience has been solo," she breathed.

Terrence's hands stilled on her calf. "You haven't?"

"You said you wanted information, and fuck, keep rubbing, and I'll give it," she breathed.

His hands continued their kneading, moving up her calf to her thighs and back down. "Who is after you, firefly?"

"You mean, besides you?"

"I'm not after you, firefly. I have you for as long as you're willing to have me," he said.

His words should have sent her into a panic, but his hands must have been magic because she arched her back to bring his hands closer to her core.

"So, if I give you tonight, you won't hunt me down tomorrow?"

"If you give me tonight, you won't want to leave tomorrow, or the next day or the next," he said skillfully, avoiding all the places she really wanted to feel his hands.

"Someone is full of themself."

"You're about to be full of me, but first, answer the question. Who is after you?"

"The entire fucking world, but you know that already. You know I'm a Phoenix, and you know how sought after my kind and our powers are," she said.

"The world can't have you. Not while I'm living and able to protect what's mine," he growled.

"Again, with the mine bullshit. I never would have nicknamed you beast if I'd known you'd start acting like one," she grumbled.

"I was a beast before you, but now I'm your beast," he clarified, sliding his hand up to tease the juncture of her groin and thigh but avoiding the most precious and sensitive part. "Now, answer my questions. The sooner we get through this, the sooner I can give us both what we need."

Cerrita wanted nothing more than to give in to the fires of arousal burning inside of her, burning between them, but she knew answering his questions would put a blanket over the whole affair. She didn't want to stop, didn't want the sweet intensity between them to end, but once again, reality wasn't on her side. She forced herself to sit up but left her legs in Terrence's lap.

"Desmon Burrage. He's the one who is after me. He's the one who set the fires. He wanted to drive me out of hiding, and it worked. The fire at my house was a warning."

"A warning of what?" Terrence said through clenched teeth. The heat radiating from him was no longer one of arousal but one of anger.

"That he's done chasing me. He was saying there was no place left for me to hide from him," she explained.

Terrence placed her feet aside before standing and beginning to pace. "Where is he now?"

"He was at my house, waiting in the fire. He's a Phoenix too. The flames wouldn't have hurt him or me."

"What about your family? Did he hurt them too? Is that why you are on the run?"

"No, they support his claim on me, encouraging it, along with my Pack. You know how valuable one Phoenix in a Pack is, but having two? A male and a female, a pair?" Cerrita didn't have to finish her sentence; she saw the moment it dawned on Terrence like a pile of bricks hitting a stuffed animal. His body literally sank right back onto the couch with her.

He ran his hand over his head before digging his phone out of his pocket.

"Tell me how we kill him," he said.

"If I knew how to do that, I would have done it by now. I've been searching for a way to end this but the Phoenix tome was no help. All it would show me was mating practices. Like a slap in the face, saying my only hope would be to surrender to him. My destiny as a female Phoenix."

"Fuck that. The only person you're mating is me. When you're ready, of course." he added the last part quickly, his eyes meeting hers. She could see his sincerity, and that only made her wish things were different. That she was just some rogue shifter without all the baggage, one who could easily return his affection. One who could mate with him without fear of being stolen away by her own personal boogeyman or worse, the actual boogeyman.

"He saw me with you in the parking lot. That's probably what sent him over the edge," Cerrita admitted.

"He was there, and you didn't tell me?"

"He's been following me since the market this morning."

Terrence's body literally vibrated with rage. He was off the couch once again, putting space between them, and Cerrita didn't like it one bit.

She'd finally found a man who didn't make her want to run, who made her feel safe and secure enough to let go, even if it had taken some convincing. She couldn't let Desmon ruin this for her. Not now, and not ever again. She reached into her duffel bag and pulled out her phone. An untraceable phone DJ had helped her procure, and dialed Desmon's number. He wouldn't have changed it. He would want her to be able to reach him if she were going to surrender to his will.

"Who are you calling?" Terrence asked, but Cerrita put her hand up to shush him.

Desmon had obviously been waiting on her call; the first ring barely finished before it connected.

"Are you done playing games?" Desmon asked.

Just the sound of his voice sent ice running down her spine.

"Fuck yeah, I am. I'm done playing your game, Desmon. I don't want you, and I never will. I've found a life here. It's time you found your own somewhere else. Somewhere far the fuck away from me."

"You've gotten yourself a nice little potty mouth, princess. I can't wait to hear more of it when I claim you once and for all," he said.

"There is nothing to claim. I'm taken."

"You mean that poor little puppy dog that's been following you? I know he's new in your life. No time to be any real threat."

"He's my mate, my fated mate," Cerrita clipped out.

There was silence on the other end before Desmon spoke again; this time his voice deadly cold. "I'm your fated mate! I am your fate! Stop this now, while I still hold some softness toward you!"

Cerrita opened her mouth to reply, but a fuming Terrence snatched the phone out of her hand.

"Listen close, you psychotic motherfucker. My mate is no concern of yours. You, however, won't escape me or the world of pain you'll experience at my hands for what you've done to her."

Cerrita should have been frightened by the pure unbridled rage that had Terrence literally foaming at the mouth as he spoke, but the diamond hardness of her nipples and the slip and slide of her lower lips told her otherwise.

She couldn't hear what Desmon said next, but the sudden roar of fire in the fireplace that sounded faintly like terrified screams was a sure sign that whatever was said had to be truly awful. She reached over and touched Terrence's arm. It was hot to the touch, so hot that if she weren't a Phoenix, it would have burned her. Because she was a Phoenix, it only made her want to mingle her fire with his. For a brief moment, she wanted to know what the fires of Hell would smell like compared to her Phoenix flame.

"Let the hunt begin," Terrence snarled into the phone before it burst into flame, turning to ash within seconds. Terrence closed his eyes, his hand finding hers. He held it while he calmed down, or rather, simmered down. The fires of Hell in the fireplace subsided, and he opened his eyes to show her the flames burning inside.

"I need to update my brothers on this situation, but first." He pulled her from the couch and into his arms before slamming his lips to hers.

Cerrita moaned, wrapping her legs and arms around him as he carried her further into his house.

"Did you mean it?" he asked as he opened the door to his bedroom.

"Mean what?" Cerrita asked, grinding her hips along his abdomen.

"What you said about me being your mate, your fated mate?" He placed her on the bed before undoing the row of buttons at the front of her shorts.

Cerrita hadn't, not really. She'd been desperate to get Desmon to leave her alone, but then she'd seen Terrence go full beast mode and her heart had gone all aflutter. He yanked her shorts and panties down her legs in one fell swoop.

"Answer me, firefly."

"Cerrita," she said instead.

"Huh?" His face was mere inches from her dripping wet pussy, and the puff of air that accompanied his confused response had her arching closer to his lips, desperate for contact.

"My future mate should know my real name," she breathed, and as a reward for her answer, he gave her sensitive flesh one long, stiff lick.

"Fated, Cerrita. Fated mate," he breathed before diving back in, licking and sucking and teasing until she was gripping his head, holding him right where she wanted him as she rode his face and tongue to the most earth-shattering orgasm she had ever experienced.

"Beast!" she screamed over and over as wave after wave of pleasure crashed over her. When she finally relaxed, her body felt wrung out and tingly at the thought that this was probably just the first of many mind-blowing orgasms she was about to be on the receiving end of. Terrence climbed up her body and placed a sloppy kiss on her lips.

"Where do you want my mark, firefly? Someplace where everyone will know you're mine or someplace only we'll know?"

Her post orgasmic bliss had her seriously contemplating letting him mark her wherever he wanted, but she knew it wouldn't feel right until this whole Desmon thing was behind her.

"Scent mark only for now."

"So, you are open to me physically marking you? I know most modern shifters aren't into the old way, but I was raised in Hell. We live and die by the old ways down there, and I couldn't risk bringing you to meet my fam without it," he said, continuing to kiss along her throat and jaw. His hand slid between her wet folds, teasing her sensitive flesh.

"You are missing the point. I can't let you mark me until this whole thing is finished. I want a fresh start. I can't be all in with one foot still in the past."

Terrence pressed one thick digit inside of her, testing her depths.

"Then I better make sure my scent mark is strong as fuck before I go kill your stalker. Anything off limits I should know about before we get started?" he said, stretching her further with a second digit. "I... I... Fuck, I'll tell you when we get there." Her pleasure had already built to a nice crescendo as he pressed his thumb against her clit and his pinky brushed against the puckered rim of her ass.

"Seems like we won't have anything to worry about," he chuckled, pressing the tip of his pinky in. It stung, but in the most glorious way, and she bore down so she could feel more of it, deeper.

"Oh fuck," she breathed as another orgasm quickly blossomed in her ass before spreading up into her pussy.

Terrence slid back down her body and covered the top of her mound with his entire mouth, his tongue taking over where his thumb had been. Sending her orgasm into hyperspace. Cerrita's brain couldn't comprehend how it was even possible that with two orgasms under her belt she wanted more.

If Terrence had ever wondered what heaven was like, he didn't need to wonder any longer. Cerrita in his bed, screaming his name, taking all he had to give, was his own personal heaven. So far, he'd made her orgasm while she rode his face, then again with a combination of his fingers, and again with his fingers while she rode his tongue once more.

He wanted to give her more, but he knew her limit was approaching. Hell, his limit was approaching. His dick was rock solid, aching, and leaking pre-cum in his pants. The one-eyed serpent was becoming impatient, but Terrence had all the time in the world to hear Cerrita's soft moans and pleasure-filled cries. He loved it when she called him beast, but when she came on his cock, nothing would do but his real name from her sweet kiss-swollen lips.

He forced his body away from hers, her soft mewling protest almost doing him in, but he was determined. He wanted to be naked with her, to feel every inch of her skin on his. He hadn't been lying when he said he wanted her scent all over his skin, that he would bask in it, roll around in it until her scent was indistinguishable from his own.

He made quick work of his clothes before settling his body on top of hers. Palming one of her small breasts, he slipped the whole thing into his mouth, massaging the nipple with his tongue until he felt her arousal dripping down his thighs.

"That's it, love, I need you ready for me," he moaned before switching to the other breast.

"Please," she begged, her tiny hips grinding against his thick thigh.

He'd gladly let her get off that way another time, but for now, he needed to be inside of her.

"Don't worry, Cerrita. You'll get your orgasm, but I need you to promise me something first."

"Anything," she breathed.

He chuckled, knowing she was too high on orgasms to make any real decisions, but he liked her this compliant and vulnerable for him, and he hoped he lived up to her trust in him.

"Call me beast all you want, anytime you want, except for when you are coming on my cock. I need to know that you know who is giving you that A plus dick."

"Fuck, I'll call you whatever you want. Just fuck me already."
Terrence smiled before positioning himself at her core.

"What's my name, Cerrita?" he said while sliding inside.

"Terrence Motherfucking Shaw," she moaned, her tiny hands digging into his hips, pulling him closer, deeper, until their pelvic bones touched. She shook all over, her inner muscles quivering on the verge of orgasm, and all he'd done was slide inside.

He took a moment to catch his breath, her hot slick walls were milking him so right and he was so hard that if he moved an inch, it would be all over, and he'd have betrayed her trust in him to give her exactly what she needed.

"That's right, Cerrita. Never forget who this pussy belongs to," he said before sliding out and slamming back in.

He fully expected her to balk at his words, but she kept rocking her hips, rubbing her clit along the length of him with each thrust. His thighs quivered as electric heat concentrated in his dick.

Her inner muscles squeezed him tighter, pulsing rhythmically and massaging him so good, Terrence wasn't sure he'd be able to hold on much longer. He didn't need to. The spasms intensified as Cerrita cried out, "Oh, oh, oh shit, Terrence!"

He may have still been able to control himself, if not for her tiny fingers digging into his ass, guiding him to faster, harder thrusts. Her closed eyes flew open, but instead of the warm brown depths he was used to getting lost in, a rim with golden flames danced inside. A ripple of feathers passed along her entire body before sharp claws pierced the fleshy part of his ass cheeks.

The mix of pain and pleasure sent him over the edge, and it was a fucking miracle he'd been able to hold his Hellhound back from reciprocating the physical mark Cerrita had left on his body.

He collapsed on top of her, his dick still pulsing, shooting his seed inside of her. He'd been so eager to be inside of her he'd forgotten to use protection.

Another thing he'd have to discuss with her later, but right then they were both too tired to do anything more than cuddle closer and fall asleep.

Once Upon a Dream

Cerrita woke up alone. Terrence was not there beside her, but on the bedside table was a tray of pancakes, bacon, and eggs. She smiled to herself as she settled in to have breakfast in bed. A luxury she hadn't had in over five years. Something she'd once taken for granted.

Her body ached in places she hadn't been aware of before that morning, but she welcomed it as well as the slightly sulfuric smokiness that clung to her skin. The soreness and his scent mark evidence of the amazing night of pleasure she'd shared with Terrence. Her mate.

Her brain didn't balk at the thought any longer. She freely gave herself to Terrence, and he gave her all of him and more.

Just to be sure, Cerrita pinched her arm. Nope, she wasn't dreaming. She'd actually found her fated mate. Her true fated mate, and he was a badass hound from Hell, not some entitled Phoenix prick. She shook away all thought of that man. She refused to let him tarnish anything more.

She finished up her food before borrowing one of Terrence's massive shirts to wear and going to find him. She could feel he was still nearby. It wasn't until she emerged into the living room that she realized why he hadn't been in bed with her when she woke up.

Sitting on the couch with Terrence were two other massive men with a passing resemblance to her mate. They shared the same wide nose, thick lips, deep brown skin, and broad muscular build but that was where the similarities ended. Terrence was the shortest of the trio easily evidenced by the angle of their knees jutting up from the couch, the one on the left was a little slimmer than than others but not by much and his hair was cut in a high top fade that reminded her of he early 90s. He also sported a single dangling skull and bones earing in one ear. A fashion trend she detested but he kinda pulled off. The other was more militant looking, a tight fade and, stiff but impeccable posture, and creases in his jeans so sharp they might rip the leather if he moved to quick. Their conversation ceased, and three pairs of intense eyes fell upon her. She was just about to flee back to Terrence's room when he stood and crossed the room to her. She relaxed in his embrace.

"Did we wake you? Did you see the food I left for you?" he asked.

"No, you didn't wake me, and yes, the food was delicious. Thank you, but can I get my bag so I can change?"

"You want to change? You look delicious in my shirt."

"Yes, but I would like to be presentable for your guests," Cerrita said, nodding toward the two other men watching them with a mix of disgust and amusement.

"Those dirtbags? They're family. My brothers, Harvey and Sampson, but yeah, I'll grab your bag. You're needed for the next topic of our conversation, and I won't be able to focus with you dressed like that."

Terrence grabbed her bag and handed it to her, but wouldn't let it go until he'd thoroughly kissed her into a swooning mess.

"Terrence, let the girl put some clothes on. We've got business to discuss," Perfect posture said.

Terrence flicked him off and kissed Cerrita a bit more before letting her go. He playfully swatted her ass before she took off back to his room.

Part of her wanted to throw on some clothes and get the inquisition she knew was coming over, but a hot shower was definitely in order. She found the bathroom with no problem and ten quick minutes later she was done and fully dressed. Cerrita had learned to be quick about her bathing a long time ago. Bathing left her too vulnerable. The reminder of her past dampened her mood, but she still held on to hope that once this thing with Desmon was put behind her, she could start unlearning some of the things that had kept her safe but isolated these last five years.

As she headed back to the living room where her mate and his family waited for her, Cerrita checked her phone. There was a message from Fancy giving her the schedule for her retraining and a half a dozen text messages from DJ asking if she was okay before saying she was coming to find her.

Cerrita called DJ instead of replying by text. She knew DJ would want to hear from her directly.

"Girl, I'm at the front door of the location you dropped. Open up before I pick this damn lock," DJ said as soon as she answered.

Cerrita rushed to the door, but Terrence was already there. He grabbed Rita and placed her behind him before peering out the peephole.

"You expecting someone?" he asked.

"It's just DJ. She was worried," Cerrita said.

Terrence shook his head. "Go sit with my brothers. I know she's your friend and all, but I need to be sure she doesn't have ulterior motives."

"She doesn't. I trust her."

"Go sit," he said, guiding her to the couch. Reluctantly, she plopped down between the two massive men, who were apparently Terrence's brothers and the rest of his shifter enforcer team.

"I'm Harvey. The stiff over there is Sampson. Welcome to the family," Harvey said without any hint at meaning it.

Terrence went back to the door and opened it a crack. "Can I help you?"

"Yeah, you can send Rita out here," DJ said.

"I cannot," Terrence replied.

"Then move your big ass," DJ said, and pushed her way inside. Cerrita was one hundred percent sure Terrence could have stopped DJ, but he didn't. He allowed her to barge into his home with just a shrug before closing the door behind her.

"Any other concerned friends I need to worry about?" Terrence asked Cerrita.

"No, just DJ," she said.

"Just DJ," DJ mimicked. "Girl, what the fuck is going on? Your house was burned down, and now you're shacked up with the three stooges shifter enforcer squad!"

"Long story short, my ex is here. He burned down my house, and Terrence and I are a thing now."

"A thing?" Terrence and his brother said in unison.

DJ looked around the room before shaking her head. "Normally, I keep my nose out of other people's business, but I'm gonna need the full story."

"Let's not get sidetracked. What do you mean by a thing?" Terrence was clearly upset by her choice of words.

"Oh, don't get your balls in a twist. We can all smell the fucking mating in the air," DJ snapped at him.

"This is between Cerrita and I," Terrence snapped back.

"Oh, so that's your full name! Boy, you need to calm the fuck down. I've known Rita for a year and didn't know her real ass name. You're her forever boo. We get it. Now, back to this whole fire thing," DJ said.

Terrence looked ready to pop a blood vessel or two, but one of his brothers stood and pushed him down into the leather recliner next to the couch.

"Chill, bro. You can have your little marital dispute after we close this fucking case," Harvey said before rejoining Cerrita on the couch. They all looked at her expectantly. With a sigh, Cerrita laid out the whole sordid tale. How her family and Pack groomed her to be Desmon's docile bride. The conversation she overheard and her trials while on the run. Halfway through the story, Terrence got up and dragged Cerrita back to the recliner with him. He held her while she recounted the whole ordeal up to the fire at her house and the subsequent call with Desmon.

"So, when are we mercing the bastard?" Sampson said.

"ASAP," Terrence said.

"Ooh, can I watch?" DJ said, wiggling with excitement.

"No!" Terrence and his brothers said in unison.

"You enforcers are no fun," DJ pouted.

"You're a civilian. It will be dangerous. Stay your ass home until Cerrita calls you," Sampson said to DJ.

DJ stopped pouting to glare at Terrence's brother. He didn't shrink under her intense glare, instead he returned it. Cerrita felt like they would glare at each other all day if she didn't step in.

"DJ, weren't you the one who urged me to get help if Desmon was dangerous? Please let them do their job. They don't need us spectating."

"Their job isn't to kill people, it's to bring them to justice."

"Pack law, but we're Hellhounds, and Hell law states an eye for an eye. Cerrita said he stole her life from her, her family. Hell law dictates that as her family now we do the same," Sampson replied.

Cerrita gasped. "Is that true?"

Terrence rubbed her back and pressed a kiss to her cheek.

"Even if it wasn't, as your mate, it's my duty to protect you at all costs. Wiping this asshole from all realms will be my pleasure."

Again, Cerrita was struck by how crazy Terrence was and how much that turned her on. Still, there was one tiny detail she had yet to mention.

"Thank you, but there's one problem."

"And what's that?"

"Phoenixes can't be killed. At least, I have yet to find a way. Otherwise, I wouldn't have run for five years hoping he would give up."

"That's not a problem at all. We might not be able to make him dead, but we can make him wish he were. Think Edi would enjoy a new toy?" Harvey said with a mischievous grin on his face.

Terrence and Sampson mimicked their brother's smile, and Cerrita suddenly got a chill. She did not know who Edi was, but they couldn't possibly be a well-adjusted therapist or anything of that sort.

"Sampson, you call Edi and give her the heads up. Harvey, you find a secure location that won't raise red flags with the human media. Rita, I need you to give me that creep's number, and then I need you to go with DJ to the Pack and tell them you are ready to be under their protection," Terrence barked.

Cerrita opened her mouth to protest, but DJ beat her to it.

"So, you're just going to force her back into a Pack after what she just told you?"

"It's a formality. She will be able to haggle better terms if she does this before news of our mating spreads. I am part of the Pack and mating me makes her part of the Pack too. If the Alpha knows that, she won't be given a chance to negotiate," Terrence explained.

"And what about after? I'm just supposed to wait around until you contact me again?" Cerrita was tired of being the damsel in distress. Sitting around waiting to be saved just wasn't her style anymore. She thought Terrence understood that.

"I need you to be safe. I won't be able to focus if I'm worried about you during the fight," Terrence said.

"How can you be sure Desmon will even agree to meet with you?"

"He already has, love. He set the time, I'll set the place."

Terrence kissed Rita one last time before allowing her to leave with DJ. After shutting the door, he turned back to his brothers and let out a frustrated growl.

"I really want to kill this bastard!"

"And you will, over and over again, because that dumb, big bird bastard can respawn like a video game," Harvey said.

"Right, but first, I need that location. I want to scope it out myself, make a backup plan in case things go left. I talked big shit to Rita, but I've never faced a Phoenix before. I'll die protecting my woman, but I want to make sure that doesn't happen."

"It won't happen. We've got you and your mate. Edi will be ready to greet the bastard when we drag him to Hell," Sampson said.

"Good, and I know just the place. There is a nice little area of the city park that isn't all that well-traveled. I can have some company witches enchant the area to keep you hidden from private eyes while we do our business," Harvey said.

"Good, I'll get him talking. You douse him with enchanted water to keep him from flaming up the place, and maybe we can have this whole thing wrapped up by dinner time," Terrence joked.

"Sure thing, we'll hit up Yarrow Cafe to celebrate. On Sampson, of course," Harvey said.

Sampson punched Harvey in the shoulder. "Let's get this show on the road, shall we?"

Terrence nodded and grabbed his keys. He wanted this to go off without a hitch. He wanted Cerrita to feel safe to go to the next step with him. Thinking of next steps, he cringed. His brothers showing up on his doorstep first thing in the morning meant he and Cerrita hadn't had the talk they needed to have. She'd said she wanted to wait on the physical marking, and yet his ass was still sore from her daggerlike Phoenix claws. He loved knowing he was hers, but wasn't sure if Cerrita even realized what she'd done. Then there was the matter of his condom slip up. He'd never been so reckless before, and Cerrita had been so out of her mind on afterglow that she probably hadn't realized what he'd done.

He'd fix that soon, before taking on Desmon. For now, he needed to make sure he had the best chance of giving Cerrita the freedom she needed. Freedom from her torment, freedom from her past, freedom from Desmon "can't take a hint even with a full fated mate threatening to kill you" Burrage.

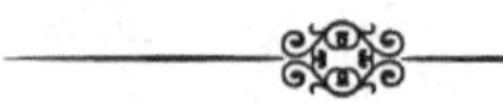

Cerrita marveled at DJ's restraint. It had been a full five minutes in her car before she asked for details about her night with Terrence.

"Spill all the tea! Is he as big as he is big? Was it everything you hoped for? How's it feel to be done with your bucket list?" DJ's questions caught her so off-guard, but Cerrita couldn't help but laugh. A nervous laugh that sounded clipped and unnatural because the significance of that bucket list being complete now weighed heavily on her chest.

"That doesn't sound good. You okay?" DJ said.

"Yeah, yeah, I just hadn't realized that was the last thing. I mean, the last thing meaning if I die..." Cerrita didn't finish the thought.

"You won't. You're a goddamn Phoenix. You will rise and rise until it is your time as told by the fates. Speaking of, is Terrence a riser, did he rise and rise to the occasion?" She chuckled at her own terrible joke. "Never mind, I know the answer. Whew, chile, I am not even a shifter and I could smell your mating through the fucking front door."

"Speaking of, I'm going to need more pheromone blocker. I don't think what I have will be enough, and Desmon torched the rest of my stash along with my house," Cerrita said.

"No worries, I got you, and while I'm making it, we can come up with our own plan. I mean, I don't doubt your new family has got things covered, but it never hurts to have a backup plan."

The urge to roll her eyes was strong. Cerrita had lived the last five years of her life as a constant backup plan. It wasn't a bad idea, but she was ready to just live her life, go with the flow, enjoy the new opportunities ahead of her. New opportunities that didn't involve being part of any Pack structure.

"Right, a backup plan that doesn't involve me going back on the run or joining a Pack just because I mated into it."

DJ's grin slipped from her face.

"Actually, that is one part I agree with your boo on. Listen, I know you have some real deal Pack trauma, but the Mulberry Pack has shown they won't treat you like the others. They allowed you to remain rogue in their territory. They didn't side with your ex, otherwise he wouldn't have tried to burn their shit down too. We'll get you that blocker, come up with a solid back up plan, and then we'll go negotiate the shit out of you joining the Pack. You're going to need their backing, eventually. It's best to negotiate when you have the upper hand. Right now, you don't need them. They've seen just how capable you are without them, and that's a bonus," DJ said.

"You sound like you've negotiated deals like this before," Cerrita said.

"I most certainly have. You've shared your life story with me. Maybe one day when you're up for it, I can share with you mine," DJ said.

Cerrita nodded. "Okay, but can we go shopping before negotiating? It will be hard for them to take me seriously dressed in this combo Hellfire uniform, yoga pants get up.

"Oh, most definitely," DJ laughed.

It took all of an hour for DJ to restock Cerrita with a new batch of pheromone blocker, as well as come up with a Plan B for handling Desmon. Terrence wasn't going to like it, but she was going to be there to confront him. She needed to see he was actually gone before she could let go of her worry.

Gather the Troops

The Enforcer Headquarters was more active than it had been in years. The frantic, hurried movements as everyone on duty rushed to get Terrence and his brothers everything they needed for tonight's showdown resembled a pack of angry bees.

"You Hellhounds are too much. You need how much enchanted water by tonight? We only just replenished our stores from last night's event."

Terrence looked up at Morgan, the Coven Enforcer Lead, and sighed, "Enough to drown a Phoenix. Call in off-duty Witches, outsource to independent contractors. Whatever you need to do, I'll make sure the council authorizes the expense."

Morgan closed her eyes and rolled her neck around. Terrence watched her hands closely to make sure Morgan wasn't putting a hex on him for putting this on her and her team so last minute. They'd done a great job of helping out with the previous fires, but this request was at least ten times larger than any before it.

"You know no amount of enchanted water will kill a Phoenix. All it does is temporarily dampen its magic, so the fire can be contained and or captured,"

"I'm aware, but we both know that as strong as me and my brothers are, a mere spritz won't cut it when facing down a psychotic Phoenix."

"The Originals should never have allowed the Phoenix line to continue. There hasn't been a single pair on record where one hasn't gone power mad. I honestly would have preferred the Phoenix line be cut over that of the Dragons," she muttered.

Terrence bit his tongue on that one. Human realm dragons hadn't been cut off. They were banished to Hell, where their greed and tempers were celebrated, but that wasn't lore he had any right to share.

"I don't care about what the Originals did or did not do. Right now, my priority is getting this Phoenix menace off the streets of Mulberry. Can you meet the demand or not?"

"We'll do our best, but short of enchanting a large lake, I can't promise it will be enough," Morgan said before storming off.

Morgan's frustration was understandable, but Terrence only had one priority and that was making sure Rita was safe. He pulled out his phone and sent her a text.

T: Have you made it to the Pack offices yet?

R: Heading there now. Had to restock on blocker.

T: Let me know when you are finished. I want to see you before tonight.

R: We are not doing the whole just in case goodbye thing.

Terence chuckled to himself.

T: Of course not.

R: Okay then, I'll have DJ drop me at your place when we're done.

T: Perfect.

His fingers itched to type more. No, they wanted to hit the call button. His gut told him he shouldn't wait to have the conversation they needed to have, but before he gave in to the urge, Sampson and Harvey walked into his office.

"Morgan hex you or something?" Harvey asked.

"No, just clarifying our order of enchanted water," Terrence said.

"So, now probably wouldn't be the time to ask her about the magical containment order?" Harvey said.

"You didn't do that yet?" Sampson scowled.

"I would have, but I needed to get the exact coordinates for the coverage area."

"That's what Google is for, takes five seconds," Sampson replied.

His brothers bickering was the last thing Terrence needed.

"Listen, I'm heading this operation. Harvey get the order in ASAP and bring Morgan a gift when you do. Sampson, have you coordinated the necessary backup?"

"Yes, I was just coming to report that this Phoenix issue has come to the attention of the council and there is some pushback on what should happen to Desmon once caught."

"Are you serious?" Terrence stood and grabbed his keys.

The council rarely got involved with their missions. Terrence knew that bringing down a Phoenix had some potential political fallout, but he wouldn't back down on making sure Desmon Burrage was never in the same realm as his mate ever again.

It was nearing sunset when Terrence showed arrived at home. Cerrita climbed out of DJ's car and met him at the door.

"You look stressed," she said, reaching up to smooth the frown lines around his mouth.

Terrence turned his head and pressed a kiss to her palm before opening the door and letting them both in.

"It's nothing you need to worry about. Everything is a go for tonight," he said.

"Is that what you wanted to talk to me about?" She dropped her new bags of clothes by the stairs as she tracked Terrence's movements. He moved more stiffly, and she wondered if last night had worn him out too much and how that might affect his abilities that night.

"No, come sit with me," he said, taking a slow, careful descent onto the leather couch.

Rita walked over and sank into his lap. "You're worrying me."

"Sorry, I just. Last night, I fucked up."

She tensed and tried to move away, but Terrence held her firm.

"Not like that. Last night wasn't a mistake. Our mating could never be. I just," he paused just long enough for the uncertainty to wrap firmly around her heart. "I forgot to use condoms. I'm sorry."

Terrence released a heavy sigh, and Cerrita stifled a laugh. He was dead serious with his concern, but the tendrils of doubt that had crept into her mind dissipated. "I know. There was zero evidence of contraception in the trash this morning, or on the floor."

While what he did wasn't okay, Cerrita knew it was an honest mistake. They'd both been wrapped up in the moment, and she hadn't exactly been careful either. Terrence held her tighter. "Are you upset?"

"If you were just some dude off the street, Hell yeah, I would be pissed, but I also would have been a lot more careful. You are my mate. If our first mating results in pregnancy, it's fine. Besides, we both got carried away last night. You forgot protection, I let my Phoenix mark you. Neither of us is innocent in what occurred last night."

"I was wondering if you remembered," he chuckled.

"My dear sweet beast, I remember everything, but if you have doubts, you can always give me a refresher," Cerrita said, moving his hand from her waist up to her breast.

Terrence smiled before trailing kisses along her jawline and neck. "I wish I had the time, firefly, but I have an important meeting I refuse to miss."

Cerrita bit her lip and rotated her hips, grinding into his lap. "You sure?"

He gently shifted her weight in his lap so she wasn't grinding right on top of his dick. She would have wiggled her way back if his next move wasn't to undo the top button of her jeans and slide his hand into her panties. His thick fingers slid along her slick swollen lower lips.

"Terrence," she breathed.

"I don't have time to replay last night, but I do have time to remind you just how good you come for me, Cerrita."

She let her head fall back, resting against his shoulder. Her hips rocked to meet the steady back and forth slide of his fingers on her flesh. He didn't penetrate her, but the steady pressure of his palm on her clit had her inner muscles dancing and desperate for more.

"Please," she moaned, arching into his touch.

Terrence chuckled before giving her what she asked, sliding first one and then another of his thick digits inside. Her greedy muscles rejoiced at having something to grip and massage and the subtle bloom of an impending orgasm made her press harder against him.

"That's it, firefly. Be a good girl, and come for your beast."

She came with his name on her lips, "Terrence!" He continued to stroke her until her spasms subsided before pulling his hand from her pants.

"We'll continue this later," he said. His voice sounded rough and almost pained as he scooted them both off the chair.

Cerrita turned and kissed him with all the pent-up desire left in her body.

"I can't wait," she said.

He smiled at her before walking out the door. Cerrita waited a few moments before pulling out her phone and texting DJ that it was time. Terrence may have thought she was content to sit back and let him try to handle Desmon on his own, but she knew he would need her help.

DJ had used her many connections to keep track of the three enforcers. The whisper network came in clutch, giving Cerrita the time and place for the showdown. After running her shopping up to Terrence's room, she changed into clothes more suitable for battle. Dark, stretchy, easy to take off, and cheap enough that she wouldn't care if they got destroyed if she was forced to shift. Then, she headed out to pick up DJ.

Sundown Showdown

"I was wondering if you were going to come." Desmon's voice carried across the small clearing to Cerrita. Terrence didn't look at her, but she knew by the clench and release of his fists he was pissed at her. Thankfully, he didn't show it. Instead, he pulled her flush against his side.

"My mate wanted you to see firsthand just how taken she is. One last chance to save yourself, big bird," Terrence said.

"Or she's finally come to her senses. You can't beat me. I'm much too powerful for you to take on your own. Cerrita knows her rightful place is by my side. Whether she comes willingly or not." Desmon shrugged. "Doesn't matter. I don't need her feelings, only her flame."

He raised his hand, conjuring a ball of Phoenix fire. The flames danced, drawing Cerrita's gaze, and she could feel it pulling at her own internal flame. Her legs started to move forward, but Terrence held her firm.

"See, she can't resist. She knows her purpose. Whether she chooses me or not, her flame will always belong to mine."

His words snapped Cerrita out of her daze.

"No! I will never give you any part of me!"

"Again, my dear, you're missing the point. I don't need you. I just need your flame. I am going to consume you, merge you into myself, so I may reach my full potential as a Phoenix and all will bow before me."

Desmon took a step closer, and Terrence pushed Cerrita behind him.

"That's a step too far," Terrence growled. He released Cerrita and charged at Desmon, but just as he's about to tackle Desmon to the ground, Desmon shifted into his Phoenix. With a curse, Terrence fell to the ground and his back arched unnaturally. Fur and fangs sprout forward and before her eyes, Cerrita meets her mate's hound for the first time. Only his attention was on the air, on Desmon, who gathered another ball of Phoenix fire intended for Terrence.

Cerrita can't let Desmon hurt Terrence. Cerrita shifted on impulse, charging at Desmon, knocking him off balance, but then he's after her. Cerrita took flight to evade him. Now in the air, Cerrita could see just how clearly they all had miscalculated. Harvey and Sampson fought off at least twenty men, some human, some not. Even though she managed to knock Desmon away, his fireball still got too close to Terrence, causing his Hellhound to yowl as the fire struck its paw. There was no way she could keep herself and Terrence safe in this place. The safest bet was to take off, leading Desmon away and giving the others time to recuperate. She'd always known it may come to facing Desmon alone, but she hoped like Hell she hadn't just ruined everything.

Terrence watched helplessly as Cerrita took off with Desmon giving chase. She shouldn't have been there. He'd purposely kept the details of this meeting from her, knowing she would try to intervene if she knew. His Cerrita was truly a sweetheart, which was what got her in this mess in the first place. The same innocence that drew him to her was the same thing Desmon had used to manipulate her for years. Terrence couldn't let her face him alone. He charged out of the enchanted circle and into the tail-end of a massive brawl. Harvey and Sampson dropped the last two goons when DJ pulled up in a small truck with a giant tank of water on the back.

"Get in, I know where she's headed. The truck won't make it all the way there, but it will get you there faster than running," she yelled out the window.

Terrence wanted to cuss her ass out. He knew she was involved with this, but at the same time, he knew she was right. So, he set his pride and anger aside and hopped into the truck, his brothers too, and DJ sped off into the park. Vehicle laws be damned.

Cerrita didn't know how much longer she could outfly Desmon. It had been so long since her Phoenix had done any kind of aerial combat, but desperation could be a potent motivator. She caught a heady air current, which zipped her another few feet in front of Desmon. His Phoenix shrieked in ire.

Please let Terrence find us.

They were on to Plan D for taking down Desmon. Reasoning hadn't helped, faking a mating with Terrence hadn't done it either, despite what her Phoenix manual had said. Although, that part had at least been enjoyable for her. So enjoyable she wasn't entirely sure their mating was fake or not. Terrence's scent still clung to her, even in her Phoenix form. It mingled with her own, creating an intoxicating perfume that was distracting, to say the least. Her Phoenix pushed harder, desperate to end this, so they could go back to Terrence and mingle their scents some more.

Cerrita knew it was a wild shot in the dark that Desmond would simply give up if he saw her happy with someone else. Desmon had chased her for far too long, he was much too obsessed for anything relatively simple to work. Plan C had been for Terrence and his brothers to corner him and bring him to justice for the fires he'd started. Only Desmon had back up that kept Terrence's brothers from getting too close. Desmon had taken to the skies as soon as he realized it was a trap.

Never in a million years had Cerrita thought about chasing after Desmon, but she couldn't let him retreat and regroup. She wasn't willing to go back on the run. Especially not when she'd found a sliver of happiness in her new life. It was only after she'd followed him away from Terrence and the others that the tables turned, and Cerrita only hoped Terrence was serious about his boasting when it came to following her scent.

Almost there.

Desmon was too focused on catching her to realize she had led him to yet another trap. Only this time, she hoped she was strong enough to make the plan work. She was drawing Desmon away from any buildings or people that would get caught in the crossfire of their impending battle. A battle where her life was on the line. Desmon had shown his hand when he thought she had mated Terrence. He didn't really want her; he only wanted her power. His detailed villain monologue was just what she had needed. The key to ending this once and for all. Desmon wouldn't be draining her Phoenix fire; she would drain him, First, she needed a safe place to do it and to give enough time for Terrence and his brothers to arrive to handle the depleted Desmon.

The thick trees below parted around the hidden marsh that came into view. Deep in the wooded area of the park, far away from prying eyes. She swooped low, skimming the water with her wings as she scanned the tree line. She saw movement along the shore, still in the trees, not quite close enough, but she was out of time. Desmon swooped down above her; claws outstretched to latch on to her flank.

Cerrita banked sharply to the left, avoiding his dagger sharp grasp, then shot straight up, looping back to divebomb him. Desmon dodged, but he was too close to the water, and his wing broke the surface of the water. He skipped across its once still surface like a skipping stone before he disappeared beneath the depths.

Yes! That should slow him down.

The water below her began to bubble and steam. Dead animals and other detritus popped up along the nearby surface as a ball of flame rose from its depths and straight in her direction.

Holy fucking shitballs!

Cerrita cursed before dodging Desmon's attack, correcting course just in time to see him emerge. His Phoenix flame danced around him in an impressive display of his Phoenix talents. Mustering all of her courage, Cerrita let her Phoenix fire dance along her feathers. Their dual flames fed off of one another as they hovered in a face off above the water. The heat coming off the two Phoenixes was so intense the water below them shrank as a steam cloud enveloped them both. Cerrita could no longer see the tree line as Desmon attempted to feed off her flame. Something she couldn't allow. She charged, but he was ready for her. Claws out, he grabbed her midair.

"You gave yourself away, you little whore! We could have had everything! Now, you'll just be another obstacle I'll destroy on my way to ultimate power," Desmon growled.

Dude was such a monologuer. Cerrita, however, didn't need to speak for her point to be made. His claws dug into her flesh; their sting intensified by the heat of his flame. She felt her own flame getting weaker as he drew on her power. She needed to turn this around, she needed to continue her fight.

"Rita!"

Terrence's bellow cut through the air. He'd found them. Cerrita gathered all of her willpower to ignore the searing pain as she flapped her wings, pushing Desmon closer to the edge. Closer to where Terrence and his brothers could help her. The steam cloud grew thicker as they approached the shore, the water shrinking below them and exposing land not seen for decades. The leaves on nearby trees browned and withered, the trunks snaping and cracking under the intense heat. Belatedly, Cerrita realized the heat of two Phoenix flames might be too much for Terrence and his brothers. Terrence had survived hers just fine, but double that was hotter than hellfire.

She didn't get a chance to ponder it long as her flame grew weaker. She would have to break free of Desmon somehow. She pushed harder, directly at one of the blistering trees. Desmon's body hit the tree with a *thunk* before the whole thing went up in flames.

"Now," Terrence shouted, just as Cerrita couldn't hold out any longer.

A deluge of enchanted water hit her, extinguishing her flame and forcing her to shift back to human form. She would have been worried if it didn't also mean Desmon was hit by the water as well. Coughing and sputtering, she crawled away from her tormentor.

"Not so fast," Desmon growled, grabbing her by the ankle. She kicked at his hand and tried to pull away. The wet, sandy mud beneath them covered her skin like a slick oil, making her escape damn near impossible. Then suddenly, Desmon let out a horrified scream, his hand dropped from her ankle, and he disappeared into the heavy steam clouds as if dragged away.

His terrified screams were joined with more wailing, and a red light appeared somewhere in the distance. A sulfureous smell hit her nose, and she knew exactly what was happening, even if she couldn't see it. Terrence and his brothers had opened a portal to Hell, and Desmon was being dragged into it. Part of Cerrita wanted to crawl closer to the light, to magic away the billowing steam that blocked her view of what was happening. Did she want to see the depths of Hell? No, but watching Desmon be dragged there for his dangerous deeds and greed would have been the highlight of her shit day. A fitting end to the bullshit he'd put her through.

Yet, she was too exhausted to do much more than wallow in the muddy puddle. The enchanted water blocked her Phoenix fire, which would have allowed her to recover faster. So instead, she listened to his screams, heard the wailing of the undead and the rumble of the ground closing and sealing Desmon away for good. The air began to chill around her, goosebumps spreading across her skin as three large canine forms emerged from the steam cloud, surrounding her. Two stopped before completely breaking the visual barrier of the steam, but the third kept coming. She fought the urge to try to flee, the overwhelming sense of foreboding washing over her in persistent waves. The beast emerged, slick black fur and sharp teeth dripping with blood. It stopped next to her before bending and licking her cheek. Terrence.

The unease she felt abated slightly, and she reached up to pet the Hellhound's head. After a few strokes, the Hellhound stepped back and shifted into Terrence's human form. He pulled her into his arms.

"Let's get you home," he said before carrying her away from the decimated marsh.

Happily Ever...

One Month Later

"I'm glad you made the decision to join the Mulberry Pack," the Pack leader said.

Cerrita didn't exactly care for the Pack leader and knew she would have to be on-guard for when he reneged on their deal, but for now, Cerrita chose to be happy. She was choosing to stick around in good old Mulberry, by her mate. Terrence stood next to her, his hand on the small of her back as she signed her name next to his in the Pack rolls. Cerrita Powell-Shaw.

"You are now recognized as a fully mated member of the Mulberry Pack," the Pack leader announced.

The Pack leader picked up the heavy tome and passed it to the recordkeeper before turning to the small group of friends and family gathered for the joint mating and induction ceremony. It was a bittersweet moment. Desmon was out of the picture, but that didn't mean that made everything he'd done disappear. Cerrita would have loved to have her family witness her mating, but the wounds of their betrayal still cut deep. That was why she didn't even think to ask Terrence to return home with her. It wasn't her home any longer. Mulberry was. Mulberry, with all its faults, had given her a new family, a family she'd chosen. One she was fairly certain she could trust, even if she couldn't fully trust the Pack leader.

As if sensing her change in mood, Terrence pulled her tighter to his side while the Pack leader gave the agreed upon speech about how blessed the Mulberry Pack was to produce such a strong mating.

"I can't wait until this is over, so I can have you all to myself, firefly," Terrence whispered.

"Me either, although, I am looking forward to tonight's PG entertainment. DJ has been raving about this new jazz singer she has lined up for tonight," she replied.

"The only thing DJ needs to line up is all of her customers, so I can clear our backlog of cases," Terrence said.

Cerrita nudged him in his side. "We agreed no talk of work tonight."

"Don't worry. I promise I am fully focused on one thing tonight."

"Oh, and what's that?"

Terrence pulled her fully into his embrace, all pretense of listening to the long winded, self-important Pack leader long gone. "You, firefly. I've got you now, and that takes precedence over everything," he said.

She smiled and pressed her lips to his, reveling in the heat building between them before whispering, "You've got us now."

"Us?" he questioned before her subtle hint sunk in. His lips parted in a full-toothed grin before he kissed her again.

Sampson knew he should have been paying attention to his brother's ceremony, but his attention was divided. He mentally combed through case files while the Pack leader continued to bloviate on the small stage set up for the main event. Sampson was happy for his brother. Cerrita was a sweet girl and deserved her happy ending. Only, now there was even more pressure to close the backlog of cases stacking up on his and his brother's desks.

With Terrence distracted, that left Harvey and Sampson to tackle the problem head on. They were the best at what they did because they were a team. Now, they were a team member short, and the stack of cases just kept getting larger. So many left open because of this new more potent pheromone blocker. A pheromone blocker created by his new sister-in-law's best friend. Disa "DJ" Jourdain was going to have to give up her client list one way or another.

Harvey was too busy running the lab to handle any field work, which left Sampson the task of convincing her to cough it up. Seemed simple enough, except as he watched DJ from across the room, the job seemed like it was about to be much more complicated than he hoped. What should have come to mind when he looked at her was interrogation and coercion tactics, not how her long sculpted legs would feel wrapped around his waist, or if her musical talents went beyond mixing others' creations, and just how many positions it would take for him to find out the full range of her talents.

Yeah, he was screwed if he couldn't put his lust in a box and carry on the mission. It may have worked out for his brother to fall for a suspect, but lightning doesn't strike twice, and if it did, it was a sign of danger to come.

Harvey Shaw slipped out of the ceremony to do a walk around the venue. One could never be too sure about safety, especially given the guests in attendance. The mating ceremony of an enforcer and a Phoenix was bound to draw trouble. Terrence may talk up his gut feelings more than Harvey and Sampson, but Harvey's gut had been telling him the trouble Cerrita had brought to Mulberry was far from over.

He pulled out his phone and dialed the one person who could put his nerves at ease.

"What!" Edi Shaw snapped by way of greeting.

"That package still sitting pretty?"

Edi sighed, and Harvey could picture his sister rolling her eyes as she used her looking glass to check on Desmon Burrage.

"Prisoner Burrage is currently receiving his spa treatment," she said.

"Good, make sure he gets the deep tissue and the hot stone. A present for Rita and Terrence," Harvey said.

"I'll make sure to add it to his treatment plan, but you might think of getting them something from the human realm. Not sure the new sister-in-law appreciates our Hell culture," Edi said.

"That why you didn't make it tonight? Didn't want to scare her off before it was a done deal?"

"You know damn well I wasn't invited," she muttered.

Harvey smiled. People assumed he and his brothers were behind the brutal rumors about Hellhounds because humans had this weird thing about patriarchy, but the real beast was Edi Shaw. The last time she was in this realm, the Mulberry Pack had nearly been exposed in her ruthless and bloody hunt of anyone connected to Kevin Kerrigan. If Harvey didn't know any better, he would have thought his sister's obsession was fueled by more than her need to bring down the biggest bad in the city. Edi might have been promoted but wasn't exactly welcome in Mulberry after her last Hellhound spree.

"Right, well, get your blood lust under control and get back here. We need you, Hellmagedon. These criminals are getting bolder by the hour with this new pheromone blocker, and Terrence is too busy with his new mate to be of any real help."

"I swear they should put mating up there with all the other brain-melting diseases to look out for. Enjoy the party, bro, but be on the lookout. I may not be physically present, but I still have eyes and ears up there. Be vigilant."

"Always," he said and ended the call.

The reminder had Harvey scanning the grounds around him once again. Nothing looked out of place, but he still couldn't shake the feeling that something bad was about to happen. Something that would change everything.

Also By Stella Williams

<u>**Sowell Gate Universe**</u>
Wild Cross Family

Felling Bechet

Yarding Braxton

Branding Baron

Reclaiming Hunter
Monsters & Mayhem

Peak
Unforgettable Contemporary

Unforgettable Valentine
Brimstone
Fire and Brimstone
Song and Brimstone
Alchemy and Brimstone
Shadow and Brimstone
<u>**Maura's Men Universe**</u>
Bloodlines

His Soul To Keep

To Catch Akellah
Secret of Ceres

Ferocious

Dauntless

Earnest

Zenith
Langsmith Shifters

Coy Wolf

A Night Divine

Bird of Prey
Maura's Men

Xander's Claim

Claude's Conquest

Shane's Redemption

Stella Williams

Stella Williams is a Blogger and USA TODAY Bestselling Paranormal Romance & Urban Fantasy Author, who lives in Washington State. She has a degree in Anthropology from The University of California, Santa Cruz. Stella prides herself in using her studies to create diverse worlds and characters for her novels. You can find more about Stella Williams on her website: www.stellawilliamsauthor.com